Dancing with Mr. Darcy

Dancing with Mr. Darcy

Stories Inspired by Jane Austen
and Chawton House Library

COMPILED BY SARAH WATERS

HARPER

NEW YORK · LONDON · TORONTO · SYDNEY

HARPER

This book was originally published in 2009 in the United Kingdom by Honno.

DANCING WITH MR. DARCY. Copyright © 2010 by Honno. All rights reserved. Printed in the United States of America. No part of this book may be used or reproduced in any manner whatsoever without written permission except in the case of brief quotations embodied in critical articles and reviews. For information address HarperCollins Publishers, 10 East 53rd Street, New York, NY 10022.

HarperCollins books may be purchased for educational, business, or sales promotional use. For information please write: Special Markets Department, HarperCollins Publishers, 10 East 53rd Street, New York, NY 10022.

FIRST EDITION

Library of Congress Cataloging-in-Publication Data is available upon request.

ISBN 978-0-06-19906-2

10 11 12 13 14 ID/RRD 10 9 8 7 6 5 4 3 2 1

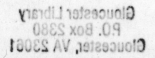

CONTENTS

Dancing with Mr. Darcy

FOREWORD

From *Bridget Jones's Diary* to Bollywood's *Bride and Prejudice*, from the Regency-horror mash-up *Pride and Prejudice and Zombies* to the forthcoming sci-fi film *Pride and Predator*, it seems that Jane Austen's work is being appropriated by contemporary culture in ever more playful and creative ways. The fact that most of the modern interest in Austen converges on just one of her novels, however, suggests that the role she plays for us might actually be dwindling, even as her presence around us seems to be on the increase. It's as if *Pride and Prejudice* has become a sort of shorthand for a whole style of literature, distracting us from the range and depth of its author's work, and offering us instead a cartoon Austen, a thing of fussy bonnets and silly manners, easy to pastiche. When I was approached by Chawton House Library and invited to judge the final stage of the short-story competition which formed the basis for this anthology, I was delighted, but also trepidatious – fearful that I would find this cartoon Austen reproduced in the stories I was asked to judge; that I would encounter nothing but Elizabeth Bennets engaged in perpetual pallid dalliances with cardboard Mr Darcys.

But my first glance at the longlisted entries was reassuring: I saw some startlingly unAusten-like titles, and an impressive array of settings and styles. In fact, so individual did the stories prove to be, the process of assessing each against its competitors became a highly challenging one. Feeling I needed to lay down some ground rules, I decided on three main criteria. First, it seemed to me that I had to be looking for something well written – a concept which, I fully understand, can mean different things to different people, but which for me meant something written with flair, by an author with an obvious talent for putting words together; but something written with skill and confidence, too – something to make me feel that, as a reader, from the first word to the last I was in good hands. Second, since this was a short-story competition, I also wanted to see stories really working *as* stories: there were some lovely pieces of writing that I rejected, regretfully, because they felt to me like fragments of prose, rather than the well-crafted, self-contained structure I felt a good short story should be. And finally, since this was a *Jane Austen* short-story competition, I wanted the stories to have some really meaningful connection with Austen herself. I was pretty flexible about this. As far as I was concerned, the connection might have been a very obvious engagement with the novelist, her work, her Chawton home or Chawton House Library; or it might have been something much more abstract; but I felt it needed to be *there*.

Each of the stories selected for this anthology meets all of these criteria: each is well written and well crafted, and between them they use Austen and her work in diverse and quite fascinating ways. A few are directly inspired by Austen's texts – 'Somewhere', for example, teases out a new story from between the lines of *Mansfield Park* to give us a poignant study of compromise and loneliness. Others are true to the spirit rather than the letter of Austen's novels; none is 'romantic' in the conventional sense, but many show youthful protagonists dealing with desire and attraction – suggesting that, although young people in the twenty-first century have the kind of social freedoms that would have been unimaginable to their Regency counterparts, love and courtship remain thrilling but difficult to manage. Still others reflect on the meaning of Austen for her modern readers – with both 'Snowmelt' and 'Cleverclogs', for instance, in different ways testifying to the power of reading itself, and reminding us of the continuing importance, in our noisy, crowded world, of the quiet, solitary spaces in which literature can be prioritised and savoured.

Given the strength and range of these and the other short stories gathered here, I found it very difficult to choose a winner and runners-up. But three stories kept drawing me back. 'Jayne' appealed to me right from the start. I liked its economy, and its irreverence, and the thoughtfulness with which that irreverence is underpinned – for though the world of its glamour-model narrator might at first glance seem far removed from that of Austen's decorous heroines, Jayne's grip on female economic realities, and on the strategies available for negotiating them, is actually thoroughly Austenesque. I found myself haunted, too, by 'Second Thoughts', an ambitious story, told from Austen's perspective and in the idiom of her novels, which attempts to bring to life an agonising moment from the novelist's own romantic career. The result is a deceptively spare piece of writing, beautifully crafted and paced, infused with real emotional power.

These two stories make very fine runners-up indeed, but it was 'Jane Austen over the Styx' that I finally chose as my winner. It's another story which attempts, and succeeds in, the tricky business of emulating Austen's voice – this time, to take us on a fantastic journey into Hades, where the novelist is judged by a panel of aggrieved female characters from her own books. It's a story with a shape, a craft; a purpose: a memorable piece of writing, engaging stylishly and intelligently with Austen's fiction and reputation.

What all the stories in this anthology show, in fact, is the continuing resonance of Jane Austen for modern readers and writers. None is a simple homage to the novelist, but each, in a sense, is a celebration of her work; and collectively they lead us back to her with fresh eyes. It was a pleasure to read and to judge them.

Sarah Waters
June, 2009

INTRODUCTION

Falling in Love with Jane

I fell in love with the novels of Jane Austen when I was thirteen. I remember sitting in a 1950s prefab that was more greenhouse than classroom. We had wooden slanting desks, the inkwells stuffed with gum and chewed paper. I would have loved a proper inkwell with proper ink. The school was in Dorking, and the view from the playing fields was of Box Hill. That was the only picturesque element. There was no Mr Darcy. I don't know if the boys were reluctant to dance as I didn't go to the discos. I do remember their bobbly nylon blazers, and how skilled some of them were in the trapping and torture of wasps.

There was a Wickham, a disreputable ginger tom who moved in with my family. We never knew his real name. One day he disappeared (eloped? off with the militia?) leaving me with nothing but rings of flea bites around my ankles. I told people that they were mosquito bites, hoping to give myself the glamorous aura of a girl whose family took foreign holidays during term-time. These were difficult years. We understood only too well the precariousness of some Austen heroines' situations.

It is the appeal of her heroines that makes Austen's work so enduringly popular. She challenged her readers by offering them characters and heroines who were not always immediately engaging. Many of the competition entrants sought to give voices and new destinies to some of the less appealing or more minor characters. There were hundreds of entries. Reading them was a delight; choosing a shortlist was horrible. Fanny Price, Mary Bennet and Miss Bates (or later incarnations of them) proved to be very popular subjects. I particularly liked a story in which Mary Bennet had a happy ending as a seafarer. I wondered whether the writer of that one had once wished she was Lizzy, but feared that she was more like Mary; I know I did.

The love and appreciation of Austen's works is evident in the stories collected here. I applaud the winner, Victoria Owens, for having something critical to say, something that goes beyond cap doffing.

So here they are – twenty stories inspired by Jane Austen or Chawton House Library. Let the love affair continue.

Rebecca Smith
June, 2009

JANE AUSTEN OVER THE STYX

Victoria Owens

JANE AUSTEN OVER THE STYX

✤

Victoria Owens

Travelling to the infernal regions was easy. True, the ferry leaked and the water seeping in through the planks of the hull was dark and cold, but remembering the hardships her brothers must endure in the navy, Jane decided to make light of it. Anyway, she did not think the ferryman would pay much heed to the remonstrations of a lone passenger like herself.

When she reached her destination and disembarked, the long terraces laid out upon the slope above the fiery lake put her in mind of Bath. The climate of the place was mild and the prospect of the distant hills pleasing. Provided that the society was pleasant she could, she thought, reside here with much happiness.

Before she could settle she had, like all mortals, to answer the charges brought against her in the court of the dead. Entering the half-timbered courthouse and making herself known to the phantasmal usher who greeted her, she reminded herself that she was hardly likely to find herself acquitted on all counts. There was no denying her life had had its faults: that tendency to be sharp, especially with her mother; the occasional fruitless burst of resentment at the good fortune of others; and of course that wretched business when she had accepted Mr Bigg-Wither's proposal of marriage only to change her mind twelve hours later. True the two of them would never have fadged, but it might have caused him less hurt if she had been plain from the outset. On the other hand, she was no Medea, nor Lucrezia Borgia, nor yet adulterous Lady Coventry. She had lived within her means and although she had sometimes been short with her family, in truth she loved them well. Had she not taken every care of her sickly mother, even when they both knew the sickness had no existence whatever outside the patient's fertile fancy?

The usher led her into an oak-panelled room with a gallery at one end and a low dais at the other, on which sat the three austere gentlemen who made up death's tribunal. For a second, she stood quite still, amazed to see how much the exercise of eternal justice resembled the workings of English law – one of those three presiding judges had even extracted a large bone snuffbox from the folds of his gown and was offering it to his companions before helping himself to a liberal pinch. The sight comforted her; she knew several snuff-taking gentlemen and found them in the main genial and warm-hearted. What had she to fear?

Fingers, bony and cold through her woollen gown, pushed her in the small of the back. The spectral usher was thrusting her with no great civility towards the dock. Disliking his prodding, she entered it at once. The wooden surround reached almost to the level of her eyes – she was not a tall woman – and she found herself surveying the courtroom from behind a row of iron spikes. Her confidence began to sink. In this setting, everything must point to her guilt before the hearing began. But guilt upon what charge? What indictment did she face? Deliberately she stared across the court to get the measure of the prosecution.

Where she had expected to meet her mother's acid eye, deep-set in the folds of her face, or hear poor, good Harris Bigg-Wither stammer out his grievance, instead she beheld no fewer than six women. Theirs were not faces of women whom she remembered from her childhood in Steventon, nor yet from the Chawton years, and she did not think they belonged to Bath. At the same time, she knew she had seen these fighting chins before. Musing, the truth dawned. The prosecuting counsel were her own creations – Mrs Bennet, Lady Catherine de Bourgh, Mrs Ferrars, Mrs Churchill, Lady Russell and Mrs Norris, whose sharp elbows had thrust her to the fore.

A black-clad clerk rose from his seat at the foot of the dais.

'Prisoner in the dock, what is your name?'

'Jane Austen, sir,' said Jane crisply.

'Kindly address your replies to the bench, ma'am. Well, these ladies,' he nodded to the prosecution, 'have summoned you here to answer a serious charge: namely, that you, Jane Austen between the years 1775 and 1817 did maliciously undercut the respect due from youth to age, in that when you created female characters of advanced years, you wilfully portrayed every one of them as a snob, a scold, or a harpy who selfishly or manipulatively interferes with the happiness of an innocent third party. Do you plead guilty or not guilty?'

She was by inclination truthful – in death as in life, but to give an honest answer was unthinkable. At the same time, the thought of having to lie brought on a rush of confusion. Now, as they stared down at her, their faces inert and colourless, the judges no longer looked so benign. What sentence might they pronounce? Prison? One of her aunts had gone to prison for stealing a piece of lace, and a miserable time she had had of it. That had been in Somerset. Although this place appeared orderly, she did not think its prisons would be as comfortable as those of Somerset, nor yet so civilised.

'Not guilty,' she replied.

'Counsel for the prosecution,' the clerk glanced at the terse old women, 'outline your case if you please.'

There was a brief babble, an altercation involving Lady Catherine, and then the mistress of Rosings deflated unsteadily upon an upright chair and Mrs Norris, adjusting her bonnet, stepped forward.

'Your honours, the facts of the case are simple. The issue is that nowhere in her clever books does the irresponsible female in the dock portray elderly women in any true light of kindness.

'Look at us. Here is Mrs Bennet who always worked hard for her daughters but who emerges in Miss Austen's writing as foolish and noisy; devoted Mrs Ferrars is made to look grasping, her friend Mrs Churchill self-absorbed and demanding. The worthy Lady Catherine, so interested in young people's welfare and so conscientious in setting their feet upon the right path through life, she presents as misguided and supercilious. She would have us believe that even beneficent Lady Russell cared less for her god-daughter's happiness than for her own. There, your honours, would I rest my case, except that I cannot forbear to remind you that my creator has the temerity to suggest that the true devotion I showed my niece Fanny Price – making her aware of her lowly station, impressing upon her the virtue of frugality, reminding her of every Christian's call to humility – was no more than crabbed meanness. Here is pure malice. And she directs all her hostility to women who are old. Female kindness and liberality, according to Miss Austen, are youth's province alone.'

'Your evidence?' enquired the judge on the left-hand side.

'In these wretched books,' Mrs Norris asserted, producing the familiar volumes from her reticule and holding them at a distance from her face as though the pages gave off a bad smell. 'For youth, Miss Austen makes every allowance. Her young women – Elizabeth, Elinor, Catherine and all – have ready charm. Anne Elliot, who is not old so much as faded, proves wiser than her father. The benevolence Emma Woodhouse shows her father counterpoises her impudence and arrogance. Mary Crawford may flirt where she should preserve decorum and speak lightly where she should be reverent, but Miss Austen tempers her impropriety by indicating the kindly fellow feeling she bears both towards her sister and, on occasion, to Fanny.

'Pray where does Miss Austen ever show a woman who is at once old, virtuous and wise? I contend, nowhere. Is not this omission a gross calumny upon the worthiest of our sex?'

'Would it be fair to add, ma'am,' the right-hand judge surveyed Mrs Norris through a pair of wire-rimmed spectacles, 'that Miss Austen is not entirely gentle in her dealings with old men either? Mr Woodhouse's extreme preoccupation with his health is perhaps less than edifying, and the gluttony of Dr Grant nothing short of contemptible. But neither gentleman lays charges against her. Is it really worth coming to court for the sake of Miss Austen's teasing?'

'But—' all six accusers rose protesting and Lady Catherine's voice carried through the court. 'Do not trifle with us, sir. You would not say such things if you were a woman.'

With a sigh, he subsided, but no sooner had he leant back than Jane found his colleague in the middle of the dais addressing her.

'Well, Miss Austen, you've heard the prosecution's evidence. What have you to say?'

These ladies – their bodies either stiff inside their corseting or else fleshy and sagging under their righteous fury – ought to make her laugh, not tremble, but when she rose to reply she found her knees were not quite steady and she had to grasp the dock's wooden surround to stop her hands from twisting together in alarm. Taking a deep breath, she made herself speak slowly as though she were calm.

'Ladies, your indignation is great indeed. You accuse me of having defamed you. But I repudiate your charge. When I wrote *Emma*, did I not take my impetuous heroine to task for her thoughtless behaviour? When my Mr Knightley asserts that Miss Bates's age and indigence should arouse Emma's compassion, not her flippancy, do I not speak out on behalf of every old woman who has ever found herself a target for youth's barbs?'

'Not so, dear.' Lady Russell had risen. 'For the fact is, your creations enjoy a more vigorous life than the sentiments they utter. We all admire Mr Knightley's integrity, but actions speak louder than words. In preparing to come to court, I had to remind myself of what he says that day on Box Hill. My memory requires no such prompting to recall how my friend Mrs Norris refuses to let Fanny have a fire to warm that chill East Room. Further, I cannot set eyes on a green baize surface without recalling Mrs Norris's effrontery in appropriating the curtain intended for the Mansfield theatricals. You may claim that respect is our due, but so often you show us forfeiting it by our conduct.'

'Is this assertion true even of Mrs Jennings?' Despite the deep breaths, her question came out in a gasp.

'Mrs Jennings who pours heartbroken Marianne Dashwood a glass of Constantia wine because it helps soothe colicky gout? Now really, that is as much a blending of the good and the ridiculous as anything you achieve with Miss Bates. Mrs Jennings doesn't help you at all.' Lady Russell's voice became stern. 'When, in the future,' she asserted, 'Mr D.W. Harding of London University will come to join us here, he will seek to convince you that in your heart you hated – his word, dear, not mine – your society and that in order to make your life bearable, you regulated your hatred by turning it to ridicule. Now, none of us much cares to be made to look ridiculous. That is why we press our charge and ask the judges of the dead to punish you by consigning your books, your letters and all evidence of your writing to Lethe. When everything is forgotten, we shall consider ourselves vindicated.'

Forgotten? When those works were so dear to her? Even if she could not refute the charge, surely she might frame some plea in her own mitigation? If she might only return to earth once more, she would create an elderly woman who combined such benevolence and sagacity that the whole world would love her and long to be as old and as clever and as kind as she. Jane opened her mouth to speak.

'Silence,' announced both the usher and the court clerk in the same second, and the judge at the left-hand end of the dais rose with upheld hand.

'Before the bench pronounces judgement,' he said, 'it behoves us to consider our powers. To suppress these books through all eternity when they stand published by Mr John Murray in elegant demi-octavos and when some of them have attracted the favourable opinions of royalty, no less, is quite beyond our remit. The court's learned advisers, Mesdames Clotho, Atropos and Lachesis, have already shown us future generations enjoying them. Sit down, please, Mrs Ferrars. Even the judges of the dead cannot fight fate.

'But neither, prisoner in the dock, can we acquit you of the charge that Mrs Norris and her co-prosecutors bring. However we have, we believe, found a way forward. Your books, Miss Austen, shall be spared and read until the end of time.'

She closed her eyes in relief.

'But listen, young woman,' the judicial voice went on, avuncular but resolute, 'to our sentence. You have, throughout your life, maintained regular correspondence with your brother Vice-Admiral Sir Francis Austen, have you not?'

Frank? An Admiral? How wonderful!

But—

'Yes, indeed, sir,' was all she said.

The judge nodded.

'Francis Austen we know to be fond of you. Throughout his earthly life – which will prove long – he will cherish every letter you ever wrote him.'

Every letter? There must be hundreds. She had kept no journal, but her writings to Frank served a journal's purpose. They held her innermost thoughts.

'He will often re-read them to catch in their sentences the cadence of a favourite sister's voice.'

At the thought of it, she wanted to laugh for pure pleasure.

'He knows you opened your heart to him as you did to no other creature upon earth.'

It was true. The novels were witty in their way, but all her happiest teases and shrewdest remarks lay in the letters to Frank.

'Your confidences,' the grave voice pronounced, 'will delight him all his days and bring him a little consolation for your early death. Further, he will harbour the hope that in time your letters' wisdom and shrewdness will reach and delight other readers too. But they never shall.'

He paused.

'Francis Austen's daughter, Fanny, shall burn them in bundles on her father's death. With them will vanish a fair part of yourself, Miss Austen – perhaps the pithiest, most compassionate part; the part that speaks through Mr Knightley rather than Mrs Norris. But your books shall remain. You may stand down.'

At the time, the thought of all her exchanges with Frank passing into oblivion left her wretched. As she departed from the court, she had to steel herself not to cry. But in the fullness of eternity, she met her niece Fanny under the white cypresses surrounding the Elysian Fields. She recognised her at once.

'What thought was in your mind,' she asked, their greetings done, 'when you destroyed my letters to your father?'

'Oh,' said Fanny, 'did I really do that?'

She frowned, as though scouring her thoughts. At last she sighed and shook her head.

'When I arrived in this place,' she said, 'I was thirsty and they gave me water of Lethe to drink. It is extraordinary that I should even know who you are, Aunt Jane, for of my earthly life I can remember nothing.'

My inspiration: Jane Austen is strong on rebarbative women. I wanted to show them turning the tables on her, and had a suspicion that Mrs Norris would take the lead.

SECOND THOUGHTS

Elsa A. Solender

SECOND THOUGHTS

❧

Elsa A. Solender

She had said yes. Yes, I will. She had felt his hand briefly touch her shoulder; his lips lightly graze her check. When she opened her eyes, he had turned away. Had he any notion that she had avoided his eyes?

Now all was settled between them. Watching him leave the room, she could read his satisfaction – his relief – in the spring of his step. Were he to leap up and click his heels together, she would not be entirely surprised, for he must be pleased that he had brought it off so well, as truly he had.

He was a stout young man turned twenty-one, just down from Oxford, wearing a striped silk waistcoat – a puce-and-purple striped waistcoat – poised to commence life as a gentleman of means, if not fashion. Was 'poised' the proper word? Was 'poise' indeed possible for Harris Bigg-Wither, a young man in a puce-and-purple striped silk waistcoat, and evidently in need of a wife, or persuaded that he was?

And now promised a wife: yes, I will.

Did he truly know what he was letting himself in for, she wondered, by offering for Miss Jane Austen? Had he no notion of the glint of irony lurking in her eye, the sharpness of the tongue disguised by the amiable, good-natured manners that she presented to the world? His sisters must have: they had known her forever. Alas, not even his sisters had seen the jottings that Cassandra – Cassandra alone – had read, the idle, *wicked* musings on the friends and neighbours whose antics she had observed with such shameful enjoyment and described with such relish to her sister. But he must know of the pages tucked into her writing slope which she sometimes read to friends, images of that other world that flashed in her restless brain, a world of handsome young men with clever conversation and fair young ladies who danced with them in The Dashing White Sergeant or the figures of another of the country dances that could so nicely set her free – briefly – of the conventions of her company.

She tried to recall dancing with Harris Bigg-Wither and could not.

It is done, she thought. No crying off.

Her poverty – this new sense of poverty since Papa had ceded his livings to brother James, this humiliating dependency upon the generosity and the whims of others – the indignities – the little slights – the necessary economies – all those would cease when she was Mrs Bigg-Wither, mistress of Manydown Park, an estate comparable – almost – to Godmersham, brother Edward's principal seat. No longer Miss Jane Austen, a dowerless spinster of twenty-six, but Mrs Bigg-Wither, wife to a gentleman of means – seven thousand pounds a year! A considerable man, however young, however shy, however blank his eyes at times, a friend, an old friend, comfortable, with no meanness in him that she knew. The five years between them would be as nothing – had not brother Henry and cousin Eliza, fully ten years his senior, dealt happily together?

Had Harris attended to the passage she had read to the

Manydown circle two nights before about the serious business of annuities? He had nodded, had he also smiled?

No need for Mrs Bigg-Wither to mend or patch her ageing boots or pelisse as they became worn; she could replace or discard them on a whim if she wished. What pin money she would have! Her time would no longer be at the mercy of others – only his, of course. Yet husbands might be managed. Everyone said so. She would learn the way of it, just as Mama had managed, and dear, good Papa had allowed it, and indeed there was still abundant affection between them.

What was it Papa had said of a marriage without affection?

No more requests – demands – to mind a child or fetch a shawl; no one, save her husband, of course, to rule her time. She must find a place at Manydown to write, a snug, quiet spot such as eluded her in the rooms at Bath where she and Cassandra now lived with Mama and Papa. No more mending and darning; perhaps some pretty needlework, but only if she wished it. Music. Manydown had a fine pianoforte. Yet, there would be the duties of a chatelaine, of a wife, indeed of a mother.

A mother.

She had felt nothing when Harris's hand touched her sleeve. His lips pressed dry against her cheek. She had no impulse to embrace or touch him.

'A marriage without affection can hardly be an agreeable enterprise.'

She would come to live among friends at Manydown, Elizabeth, Catherine, Alethea, the Bigg sisters, good girls, dear girls, if not clever; but they were friends, dear friends throughout the golden Steventon years. Good to her, wishing her only happiness. And Steventon, dear Steventon, so near, still home, always home, even with James and his brood occupying the parsonage.

Where amongst this lively, noisy family of Biggs and Bigg-Withers could solitude be found, a place and time to retire, to reflect and, yes, record?

Mrs Bigg-Wither of Manydown would be an instrument to relieve the trials of her parents and sister. She would be the heroine of her own bright tale. Cassie could live with them much of the time, just as she stayed often at Godmersham. And she, Jane, could advance the careers of the Austen sailors, Frank and Charles, and perhaps even poor, dear Henry whose enterprises – well, clever, charming Henry always found a way, did he not?

She must feel a kind of affection for Harris Bigg-Wither. Surely she could learn such affection. She had made a sensible choice, a comfortable choice; a choice *for* comfort. Nothing could be said against the suitability of the match despite the five years longer she had lived than he. The most critical of friends or neighbours in Steventon or Bath or even those at Stoneleigh, from whom much was expected one day, could not but approve her choice. It was a wholly practical decision, a decision greatly to her advantage, indeed greatly to the advantage of the entire Austen family. Through this alliance, she would be elevated from genteel poverty as a retired, landless clergyman's second daughter to a most enviable situation in society, comparable – almost – to that of sister Elizabeth Bridges, brother Ned's Elizabeth, whose dowry had so nicely enhanced the stature and fortune of that already most fortunate of the Austen brothers. A fine match indeed.

Why, therefore, with all the advantages of the match enumerated, does she suddenly feel a dull, heavy weight descending upon her shoulders? Why a throb of dry pain in her throat and a pressure behind her eyes? From whence come the tears stinging inconveniently behind her eyelids, threatening to flood the room? Why this sudden revulsion of feeling?

Not fair! Not fair!

Oh, Jane, you must embrace your fate, stifle your tears and hold your errant tongue. You must thank providence for your good fortune, come not a moment too soon, for at six and twenty, you are rescued and shall be elevated simply by speaking those few words: 'Yes, yes I will.'

She will bask in Mama's approval, in Papa's relief. Cassandra shall be made secure, James and Henry, even Ned, shall be relieved of her future care, and she shall be transferred from one dependency to – a kind of freedom. Perhaps.

Children. There must needs be children, and not the children of her fancy – Susan, Lizzie, Elinor, Marianne – but children of solid flesh and blood, and tears.

No time for regret, for here are the Bigg girls come into the library to embrace her as a sister and congratulate her, all smiles, on her good fortune. Cassandra, too, is here, holding back just a trifle, perhaps questioning without words, perhaps sensible of the turmoil in her mind and heart, yet not disapproving.

All of them, sisters to bride and groom-to-be, had colluded in bringing about the encounter between Harris and herself, a private moment for which poor Harris had been primed, as had she. Against such a confederacy – a campaign so kindly intended – how could the principals, so beloved of the conspirators, venture resistance?

'You will see how he has improved since he came down from Oxford,' she had been told. 'You will observe his gentlemanlike manners, the marked improvement in his address. So tall, so much slimmer now, so much neater in his person. The stammer – why, in your company, dear Jane, in the company of a friend with whom he is so comfortable, hardly a stammer at all. And with your good sense and fine taste, his improvement cannot but continue. Clever puss, you will change him, Jane, indeed you shall.'

Even a much-beloved sister, a best friend, could be deceived by the cheerful demeanour she had adopted, stifling the pangs of doubt that had begun to tease her even before they lit their candles and retired for the night.

For he is still stout. Improved, yet still raw. Callow. Nothing like some young men with whom she has danced or flirted in her time, in her *youth*. Nothing like the young men in that other world to which she sometimes withdraws, young men in whose quips and manners she has discerned a capacity for serious consideration of principles. Nothing like a certain gentleman at Sidmouth whose name may not be mentioned, whom she had met and perhaps loved, then mourned. Nothing like the clever, handsome, dashing brothers whose figures she has described and whose teachings and sayings she has recorded for use someday in as yet unwritten tales – and, yes, some she has written.

Harris Bigg-Wither has nothing to teach her. Will he ever possess the capacity to make her laugh? Has she the talent to make him laugh? Could he abide a wife who yearns secretly but, yes, ardently, for publication and acclaim? Is 'irony' a word in the Bigg-Wither lexicon? Has she the capacity, or the will, to embrace him? Can she accommodate his embrace?

Not fair! He is blameless in this affair. He is deserving of all her consideration, for his motives contain no hint of evil. Were he to be disappointed in his hopes after her assent, the fault must all be hers. The force of that argument does not elude her even as a new wave of self-reproach threatens to suffocate her.

She must wake Cassie at once. She must flee this room and this house. She must remove to some dark hidden corner of the world to shut herself away from decent society in misery and guilt. For misery is the state in which she now finds herself, awake in the darkness of this chamber.

Yes, she had said yes, and that simple word must be her undoing. All her musings on fortune, position and glory, all her ambitions must be forsaken; for she knows now that never – never in this life – can she become the wife of a man for whom she feels no strong regard, indeed no spark of true affection.

She wishes him well. She wishes him a partner worthy of his good heart and his simple, cheerful nature, one who will overlook the spots that linger on his countenance, who will not rue the vacancy of his expression when one of the company ventures a sally on the curate's sermon, nor count the endless moments before a pun is grasped or the beauty of a line of music or poetry apprehended. She wishes him a partner with no need to have her nonsense grasped and esteemed – instantly.

She must lie still and silent beside Cassandra through the rest of this dark night. She must listen in sleepless disquiet to the rhythm of her sister's even breathing. A suffering heart need make no sound. She has no wish to do a grievous injury to a worthy, innocent young man, one not at all deserving of such treatment. She must calm herself. She – fancying herself mistress of the well-turned phrase – must search for a formula by which she may unsay what she has said in a fashion that gives the least injury. She must prepare to sink herself in the regard of her friends and family and, worse, in her own regard. Whether relief or undoing awaits her with the sunrise, she dares not predict.

Upon waking, as the first glimmers of dawn sparkle through the draperies, Cassandra understands instantly. She comprehends the turmoil, the torture, the regret, all that she, Jane, had hidden before the punishment of the past night.

It is Cassandra who rings for the girl, Cassandra who relays the request from Jane for a private interview with Harris Bigg-Wither, Cassandra who begs the use of the carriage directly, without delay, to transport them from this place of disgrace to Steventon from whence brother James may see them back to Bath.

We should not suit, she tells him. I can proffer no other explanation, no other excuse. I apprehend that you have honoured me with your regard, but we should never suit. With all my soul, I wish you every happiness. You will surely find another, one day. I have every confidence that you will form an attachment with a woman more worthy, more deserving of your devotion and your goodness. I pray you will forgive my hasty assent, my thoughtless words; my stupid reply to so generous and respectable an offer, but we should not suit, truly we should not. I can only add, God bless you.

She can invent no more felicitous phrases as he regards her in dumb— *Why can she not resist that harsh word?* In *dumb* silence.

How cruel, how unforgivable to think in such terms!

A marriage without affection can hardly be an agreeable enterprise. To whom should she assign this sentiment? To Miss Elinor Dashwood, perhaps, or to the acerbic Mr Bennet, or another whose words echo in her ears, waiting to be written.

Cassandra has succeeded in begging the carriage. Their boxes are packed, her writing slope on the seat. How soon before she may record the details of this debacle before they slip from her mind? *Not yet, not yet.*

As she climbs into the carriage, she is embraced unselfishly, tearfully, by each of her friends, Elizabeth, Catherine, Alethea; their kind expressions show that they bear her no ill will. Harris has wisely absented himself from this farewell.

She does not look back as the carriage draws away from Manydown.

❧

My inspiration: My story, set before the Austen women moved to Chawton, would never have been written if I had not seen Chawton for myself. Trained as a 'new critic' focused on textual analysis, I loved Jane Austen's work but had largely ignored her life. I was unexpectedly moved seeing where she lived and wrote. I thought the intriguing blank in her life – her possible romantic and marital interests – might be credibly portrayed by a fictional foray into her consciousness that was supported by my appreciation of her style and the knowledge of her life that I acquired only after visiting Chawton.

JAYNE

Kirsty Mitchell

JAYNE

❧

Kirsty Mitchell

A large income is the best recipe for happiness I ever heard of.

I mouth the words as I lean forward. *Mansfield Park.* My nipples shine pink and hard under yellow studio lights.

'Lower, love.'

Mansfield Park. Mansfield Park, the third published of Jane Austen's novels. Or was it fourth? Shit.

'A bit to the left.'

The plastic shutter makes a loud click as it opens and shuts, and the noise rattles obnoxiously around the small studio. I try not to squint against the bright lights behind the fat photographer. The one today is particularly grotesque, with shreds of hair and a screwed-up face. I lie on a sheepskin rug and run through quotations in my head. *The mind is its own place, and in itself can make a Heaven of Hell, a Hell of Heaven.* Milton.

The photographer steps out from behind the camera and I am struck afresh by how hideous he is.

'Brilliant. Lovely. That's great. In fact,' he grins broadly, 'it's… tit-tastic.'

Oh, *fuck off*. Fuck off and *die*, you fat old perv. I smile. Think of the house, and grin and bear it. Bare it. A few years modelling, and I'll have enough to buy a flat. I'll live there a few years then get tenants in. The way the market's going, the rent should cover a mortgage on a house, maybe even a few quid in an ISA. Financial security is very underrated. Plus I'm paying for this university course, for which I can't even bloody remember the facts. I'd like to say I didn't finish school because of mitigating circumstances, family situations, but the truth is it was too much like hard work and I couldn't be arsed. Now I'm paying £200 a month for my education. As Joni Mitchell said, you don't know what you've got till it's gone. Or Shakespeare. *Nothing can come of nothing.* King Lear, Act I. Shakespeare almost made me cry before the last exam. I had a big job on the same day and I sat in the bath the night before, face mask on, mouthing the words. *To be, or not to be. That is the question. Whether 'tis nobler in the mind to suffer the slings and arrows of outrageous fortune...* a blob of strawberry and mango oatmeal scrub fell into the water.

'Can you put your arms together, love? Push them up a bit?'

I'd like to do well in the Jane Austen part of the course, because my mum's a big fan. That's how I got my name, actually.

'Jane?' they said when I was starting out.

'With a Y.'

'Jayne?'

'Yes.'

The guy frowned. 'No, that's no good for a page three. Plain Jane. No, we need something more exotic. What about Destiny?'

'No.'

'Faith?'

'No. What about Maya?' I suggested.

Maya, the Indian religious deity who represents the notion that the distinction between the self and the universe is a false one. From last year's philosophy of religion module, part II. If I was going to be named after a philosophical concept, I'd rather it was a half-decent one.

'Maya!' He winked. 'Sexy!' What a cock.

Of course Mum wasn't happy when she found out. She sat sulking in the living room. Peach-pink couch, carpet, curtains that gave everything an odd glow. There was a clashing fake brass fireplace in the middle of the room, on which fake flames swirled. Her ornaments were in a display cabinet on the back wall: a creamy porcelain mass.

'Calm down, Mum,' I said.

'Calm down?' A pink-fringed slipper hit the floor. 'Calm down? Do you think this is what I hoped for when I had you? That I looked down at my baby girl and thought, one day she'll get her breasts out for the *Sun*?'

'*The Daily Star*,' I corrected.

'*The Daily Star* then. Am I supposed to be proud of that? Bloo-dy hell.'

I looked past her frizzy head to the bookcase. All the Austen books sat there in alphabetical order. The spines were cracked and ratty. On the shelf below were the DVDs and videos, and on the wall behind was a poster of the cast of *Pride and Prejudice* that came free with one of the DVDs. She'd once got an Elizabeth Gaskell book out the library, in a plastic cover with crumbs trapped underneath, but she hadn't liked it. 'She's just not our Jane, Jayne!' she'd cried.

'I'm disgusted by you,' she said.

'Och, Mum,' I breathed.

With my first pay cheque, I bought her the complete BBC Jane Austen adaptation box set.

It's an easy job, by and large. Pouting and posing until my back aches and my skin starts to perspire under the lights and the powdery make-up. It's all smoke and mirrors.

'What do you do?' someone asked me at the uni.

'English Literature,' I replied.

'No.' He laughed. 'I mean your day job.'

'Ah,' I said. Get my tits out. 'A nurse,' I told him. I frequently am. That or in corsets. I hate the corsets. There are cold metal rods inside that press against my skin and make me ache for hours afterwards. What is it with men and bloody corsets?

I'm quite polite, as far as this industry goes. I only do the tabloids and the soft magazines. I wouldn't do any of the other magazines or any of those late night channels on freeview, the ones where girls wriggle around in cheap plastic costumes and make out like they can't wait to receive illiterate texts from wankers, when any fool can see they'd rather be at home in front of *Eastenders* with a digestive biscuit. It's still not the kind of thing to discuss at a dinner party though. I once went out with a boy who lived in one of the big houses in town, and his parents invited me round for dinner. Mum was beside herself. 'Take them a bottle of wine,' she told me. 'And don't get a cheap one. You don't want them thinking you've got no class.'

We all sat politely around the dinner table, arms straight. His mum brought out the best glasses, which sparkled against the candles. I was wearing a nice blue dress with a ribbed waist from Karen Millen.

'And what do you do for a living, Jayne?' they asked.

'I work in a photography studio.'

'Oh, very good. Is it some sort of admin job?'

'Not really.'

'More hands on, then?'

'Kind of.'

But then his dad saw me dressed up as a cowgirl in the *Sun*, and so that was the end of that.

I do get bored though. I suppose anyone does, in any job. Myself, I am so bored of tits. They're all over the walls of the studio, big ones, wee ones. Mainly big ones. They're just *tits*. There are days when I feel dismayed by the repetitiveness of it all, the stupidity. The stupid costumes, the ridiculous scenarios. Men are so easy to snare. One of the magazines I appear in sells for seven quid in the newsagents. Seven quid! *Some Cupid kills with arrows, some with traps. Much Ado about Nothing*, you know. Or was it *As You Like It*? Fucking hell.

Lunchtime. We film in a block of rented offices, a concrete, square place with a rubbish café. I go to the café, order a baked potato in a plastic box. I've brought *Pride and Prejudice* with me, the copy I use for studying: highlighted fluorescent yellow all over, the spine battered and creased.

'Hiya.'

I look up and to my irritation see the photographer's assistant sitting down opposite me at the table. We've had a few of his sort, and they're all the same. Slouchy hats, sculptured facial hair, just out of university, think they're going to end up in far-flung corners of the world shooting pictures of Aids orphans and politicians and unfortunate victims of unfortunate disasters, but instead end up in the back street of a bad area of Glasgow, shooting breasts.

'Hello,' I say darkly.

He taps my book with a long finger. 'Wouldn't have thought girls like you would—'

'What?'

He looks at me.

'Nothing.'

'What? A girl like me wouldn't be reading an actual book? What am I meant to be reading in my lunch hour, *bra* catalogues?' A couple of the office workers turn around.

He leaves. I shake the book open. Do you know, I bought a copy of *Cosmopolitan* a couple of weeks ago and they had one of those stupid foil-covered male nude pull-outs. And all the men they'd asked to be in it were doctors and lawyers and aeronautical engineers. You don't get that in any of the bloody magazines I appear in.

Sometimes they ask the girls for a comment. They always want some vacuous, dim-witted remark about some topical issue.

'So what do you think about immigrants, Maya?' the photographer asked. The eye of the camera clicked loudly, open and shut, open and shut.

'In the context of immigration or emigration?'

He looked bemused. 'Both.'

'Right. Well firstly, I think the media has vastly misrepresented the number of immigrants coming into the country, and I think the reporting has been biased. I recently bought a newspaper and there was an article about the falling birth rate in Britain and how this was going to bring everything to its knees in the future; the NHS, state pensions and so on. But on the other page there was an article about how there were too many immigrants flooding into the country. Now, to me, there's a contradiction there that smacks of racism. What they're saying is that there aren't enough *white* babies being born. If there's a demographic argument that birth rates are falling too fast, then why the hell shouldn't we be welcoming immigrants, especially those with young families? And there's a possible genetic benefit for the health of the native population as well, particularly in a place like Glasgow where a high proportion of native Glaswegians have an ingrained genetic predisposition towards diseases linked to the immune system, like heart disease. So if the two populations interbred and mingled, this could be genetically beneficial. Although naturally whether this integration did occur would be dependent on social and cultural factors. So, in short, I'm in favour of it. And I think the media has fanned the issue because it sells papers,' I finished.

He stared at me. My breasts jiggled. 'Right,' he said.

He looked disconcerted. A man like me is allowed to be intelligent, a woman is not. *A woman especially, if she have the misfortune of knowing anything, should conceal it as well as she can. Northanger Abbey.* I experienced a slight thrill at having remembered it all the way through.

Back upstairs, clothes off again. The photographer leers at me, the fat bastard. I reckon I've only got a few years left in this. The market's too competitive now. Magazines, websites, television channels—

'Only so many punters in this game, only so many wallets,' the photographer said, in a tone as close as the big ape got to philosophical.

'There certainly are not so many men of large fortune in the world as there are pretty women to deserve them,' I said.

He looked perplexed.

'*Mansfield Park*,' I told him. 'Jane Austen.'

The exam tomorrow. A drafty dusty hall, biros on the desk. I'll do the rest of the modules, finish the course; pay the fees. Buy the flat, have financial security, spend the rest of my life doing what I want to do. I'll be too old for it soon anyway, the age of some of the girls coming through. A career where a woman is worthless by the age of twenty-five. It's a disgrace.

I stretch an arm behind me, arch my back.

'That's beautiful,' the photographer says. He sniggers behind snaggled, cracked teeth. 'It's tit-riffic.'

Oh. Yuk. *Lord, what fools these mortals be!*

❧

My inspiration: Despite the fact that many of Jane Austen's novels are considered love stories, I think there's a hard, pragmatic edge in how her characters speak about class and money that is often overlooked. W. H. Auden said that it made him 'uncomfortable' to see her 'describe the amorous effects of '"brass" / Reveal so frankly and with such sobriety / The economic basis of society'. Given this, I wanted to create a character who had this same pragmatic edge about money, in a very modern day context.

THE DELAFORD LADIES'
DETECTIVE AGENCY

Elizabeth Hopkinson

THE DELAFORD LADIES' DETECTIVE AGENCY

Elizabeth Hopkinson

This was going to be a most interesting case, thought Mrs Reverend Ferrars, as her sister, Mrs Colonel Brandon, poured tea for the lady sitting nervously in the small parlour of Delaford Parsonage. So far her talents as a detective had mainly been used to ascertain the true characters of potential suitors or to assure nervous mammas that their daughters were truly engaged (although there had been that unforgettable incident with Mrs Ellis's chickens). She was looking forward to something a little more challenging.

Of course, it had come as a surprise to her to find she was a detective at all. When she had first arrived in Delaford, she had naturally expected simply to support dear Edward, take baskets to the cottages and raise a handful of plump, well-behaved children. Sadly, the latter had not been forthcoming, and while Mrs Ferrars might envy her sister the third swelling beneath her day gown, she knew better than to brood on what might have been. Occupation was a great comforter, and Mrs Ferrars had found one well suited to her temperament: People had always confided in her (in the cases of Lucy Steele and Mr Willoughby, not always with her willing agreement) and she found she had the kind of sharp mind that relished a puzzle.

'Pray, make yourself at ease, Mrs Worthing,' she said, with the reassuring smile she generally used on such occasions. 'Mysteries, I find, are rather like knots in one's embroidery thread. They may look impossible, but they always unravel in the end.'

It was important to say something like that, Mrs Ferrars found. Mystery, on the whole, was something she profoundly disliked. It had uncomfortable associations with Gothic ruins and over-emotional young ladies in white gowns. Being able to rid it from the neighbourhood was something that had encouraged her to keep going after the success of her initial case with Miss Morton's coded Valentine. Detecting was a service to society, and therefore an occupation very worthy of a parson's wife.

'Oh, do not mention embroidery thread,' sniffed Mrs Worthing, dabbing at her eyes with a lace handkerchief. Mrs Ferrars began to suspect her of sensibility or – worse still – sentimentality. 'Not when a ghostly presence comes each night to my work basket and works on my embroidery – my very own embroidery – while Delaford Park lies in slumber.'

Mrs Ferrars stiffened slightly. 'Lies in slumber,' had sealed her opinion of Mrs Worthing.

'Only think of it, Elinor,' said Mrs Brandon, helping herself to a Banbury cake behind their guest's back. 'All this time I have been living in a haunted mansion. I'm sure I shall never sleep again at the thought of something so horrid. And to think that Colonel Brandon never told me.'

Mrs Ferrars secretly suspected there was nothing her sister would like more than to live in a haunted mansion, but now was not the time to mention it.

'Oh come, Marianne,' she said. 'Colonel Brandon has enough

ghosts in his past without bringing them into his house. Have you questioned the other house guests? The servants?'

'Of course,' Mrs Brandon eyed the last remaining cake with longing. 'And they all say the same thing. No one has seen or heard anything. Only the Misses Hart do say they can feel a ghastly chill around the basket.'

Mrs Ferrars sniffed. She could imagine well enough how effective Marianne's questions had been. She looked back to Mrs Worthing with a twinkle in her eye.

'You know, you could always take your work basket to bed with you.'

'And never discover what ails the poor, tortured soul? Oh, Mrs Ferrars, do not suggest such a thing.'

As Mrs Worthing applied the handkerchief yet again, Mrs Ferrars thought of several things she *could* suggest – a more instructive diet of reading for one thing – but she resisted. It was certainly time for the light of reason to be shed on Delaford Park.

'Mrs Worthing, leave the matter to me,' she said.

The house guests at Delaford Park, although unknown to Mrs Ferrars, were not unlike the guests at any country house, and private conversation with each about the embroidery yielded only fantastical supposition on the part of the ladies (Mrs Worthing and her two rather empty-headed sisters, the Misses Hart) or total lack of interest on the part of the gentlemen. These comprised Colonel Brandon, Mr Worthing (who appeared to take no interest in anything beyond coarse fishing and eating) and an army friend of the Colonel's named Major Black, a pale, quiet man not unlike the Colonel himself. No one was prepared to offer anything useful. They had seen nothing, nor did they have any suggestions as to why Mrs Worthing's embroidery seemed to have decided to finish itself.

Mrs Ferrars hoped to have better success with Miss Amelia Black, the Major's sister. There was something in her eye which suggested rather more of quickness than the other ladies, and Mrs Ferrars was glad to approach her in the privacy of the walled garden.

'Good afternoon, Mrs Ferrars.' Miss Black looked up and curtseyed. 'Mrs Brandon has told me all about you. I am most impressed. Generally, if a woman knows anything, she should conceal it as well as she can. To make use of your intellect as you do is a bold thing indeed.'

'I only make use of it privately.' Mrs Ferrars did not wish to be thought inappropriate. 'And only in cases which concern ladies, as with this matter of the embroidery. Now tell me, Miss Black, what do you know? You do not give credence to this tale of a ghost, do you?'

'Oh, no.' There was just a hint of something in her eyes as she spoke. Perhaps fear, Mrs Ferrars thought. She had believed Miss Black to be calm and rational when she first began to speak, but now Mrs Ferrars noticed she was plucking at her sleeve, although she kept smiling. 'Perhaps Mrs Worthing completes it herself, for her own amusement.'

'Perhaps. Yes, perhaps that is it. If you are quite sure you have not worked on it yourself, or seen another do so.'

'No, not at all.' Miss Black curtseyed again. 'If you will excuse me, Mrs Ferrars.'

Mrs Ferrars now felt she had the full measure of Miss Black. She was hiding something. But that was only part of the investigation. It was one thing to discover that a person was lying, quite another to discover why or what about. And delicacy was everything. It was time to take a different approach.

She stepped towards the dovecote. 'Mrs Worthing, may I please see your embroidery?'

Mrs Worthing's embroidery was, thought Mrs Ferrars, dully unexceptional, especially considering it was at the heart of such an intrigue. She had always found white stitches upon white muslin to be particularly tedious, and there was far too much feather stitch to render it truly interesting. Mrs Worthing, however, took great pride in showing it to her.

'This part was worked by my hand. And this part,' her fingers trembled as she touched it, 'was worked by the ghost.'

Mrs Ferrars held it up to the light. She feared that she would soon begin to need spectacles. Certainly, there was a difference between the two styles. Mrs Worthing's was neat and reminded one of embroidery lessons in the schoolroom. The second hand showed more imagination, if less precision.

'And is Miss Amelia Black's embroidery close by?'

Mrs Worthing blushed at the ungenteel concept of opening another lady's work basket.

'Pray, do not stand upon ceremony, Mrs Worthing,' said Mrs Ferrars. 'You may always complain to my husband if you disapprove of my morals.'

Mrs Worthing reluctantly pointed out the basket and Mrs Ferrars examined the work within. Again, the style was different, but it did not match that of the 'ghost'. Clearly, if Miss Black did know something, she was covering for another person. With a sigh, Mrs Ferrars went about examining the work baskets of the other ladies, Marianne included. Mrs Worthing was beside herself with horror.

'If the ghost should be a lady whose work basket was once disturbed…oh, Mrs Ferrars, please desist!'

Mrs Ferrars scowled. None of the styles of embroidery resembled the second hand on Mrs Worthing's muslin. She could have Marianne question the servants again, but then there was the behaviour of Amelia Black to consider. Miss Black was unlikely to lie for a servant in someone else's household. There had to be another possibility she had not considered.

In circumstances such as these – when an investigation seemed to be going nowhere – Mrs Ferrars invariably consulted the wisdom of Dr Johnson. There were few subjects on which the learned Doctor had not held forth, and Mrs Ferrars found his influence both calming and instructive. In this instance, she recalled his words on the subject of knowledge.

'Knowledge,' Dr Johnson had said, 'is of two kinds. We know a subject ourselves, or we know where we can find information upon it.'

Mrs Ferrars considered how to apply these words to the case in hand. The only information upon the subject of Mrs Worthing's embroidery lay with Amelia Black, but Miss Black was unwilling to give it up. She must therefore seek another source of information or endeavour to know the subject herself. She closed her eyes, temporarily ignoring Mrs Worthing's gasps for the smelling salts. This was no time to dilly-dally. Common sense was at stake. She must know the ghost.

'This is so exciting, Elinor,' Mrs Brandon exclaimed, as she closed the drawing room curtain around her sister. 'I'm sure the Colonel employed spies in the East Indies, but I never thought to be doing so myself.'

'You are doing no such thing, Marianne. Spying is a most un-ladylike and un-English occupation.' Mrs Ferrars drew the thick, woollen shawl around her shoulders, wishing that night air were not so very injurious to one's health. 'I am simply resting in the window seat for the time being, as I have trouble sleeping. Naturally, you will all be in bed while I do so. It was very kind of Edward to let me stay the night.'

Kind it may be, thought Mrs Ferrars, as Marianne retired, but she was not at all sure that she wouldn't rather be in her own bed at the Parsonage with Edward than waiting on a window seat for a mysterious embroiderer. Supposing the lady in question should be of a desperate nature? No, she felt sure that anyone who worked satin stitch with such delicacy could only be respectable. She would simply have to wait and see.

A light tread in the passageway caused her to stiffen. The drawing room door was opening. A more muffled tread indicated that someone was crossing the turkey carpet. Mrs Ferrars heard the slight creak of a sofa and the rustle of a work basket being opened. Then there came a sigh, a sigh in a rather lower register than Mrs Ferrars would have expected.

She peered around the curtain. Seated on the sofa was Major Black. His lips were pursed in concentration and he was squinting by the light of a candle he had carried in himself. He was embroidering on Mrs Worthing's muslin and – as far as Mrs Ferrars could make out – doing so with considerable skill. In fact, if her examination that afternoon was anything to go by, his work was slowly transforming a dull, schoolgirl piece into something remarkably artistic.

Mrs Ferrars dropped the curtain and hugged her knees in silence. Her investigation was at an end (if an unexpected one) but she was left with a dilemma. Obviously, Miss Black did not wish it to be known that her brother secretly indulged in embroidery any more than he would wish it to be known himself. Mrs Ferrars saw no need to create social embarrassment within the Delaford household. On the other hand, she needed to lay the 'ghost' to rest before Mrs Worthing, Marianne and the Misses Hart became any more excitable. She fingered her shawl while Major Black tutted over his French knots. Perhaps there was an answer.

*

'And I hope you will allow me to make you this gift, Miss Black,' said Mrs Ferrars. 'You will know where to make the best use of it, I am sure. I have informed my sister and Mrs Worthing that the ghost will cease to trouble them in future. It is a pity I never clearly saw the person who worked those remarkable stitches. As I said to Marianne, I fear I shall soon need spectacles. But I would say they had a true talent for needlework. It would be a pity to let it go to waste for lack of a suitable outlet.'

'I'm sure I am most grateful to you.' Miss Black's curtsey covered her confusion, but there was something in her step as she left that suggested greater peace.

The parcel from Mrs Perkins' haberdashery had cost rather more than Mrs Ferrars' small allowance really stretched to, but it was worth it. If Major Black wished to pursue his embroidery, then having materials of his own would make it much more convenient. She was sure his sister would know how to make the gift in a suitably discreet manner.

Of course, Mrs Worthing and Marianne were still not entirely satisfied with Elinor's report that she had seen nothing whatsoever but was convinced that the ghost would leave within two days of all the ladies taking up an instructive course of sermons and essays.

'There's still an air of mystery about this,' Marianne had insisted in whispered tones over breakfast.

Still, that was nothing that a private word with Colonel Brandon could not ease. It was not inconceivable that he had some idea of his former subordinate's skill with a needle. And when she impressed upon him the fact that mystery was, of all things, the most damaging to his wife's health in her condition, she felt sure he would lay down the stamp of reason as firmly as could be wished for.

It was a debatable conclusion, thought Mrs Ferrars, as she arrived back at the Parsonage, to be greeted by a kiss from Edward and a tirade of questions from the maid about the best way to restore fine lace. There had been some deceit involved, which she was not sure was fitting for a parson's wife. But then again, order and reason had been restored and reputations saved, which had to be a good thing.

She turned over a page of Dr Johnson's works that lay on her small table.

'What then is to be done?' she read. 'The more we inquire, the less we can resolve.'

True, thought Mrs Ferrars, but she relished the challenge of inquiring nonetheless. That was what being a detective meant.

⁂

My inspiration: Elinor Dashwood seems to be surrounded by mysteries and people telling her their secrets, so I thought it would be fun to cast her in the role of a detective and cross *Sense and Sensibility* with *The No 1 Ladies' Detective Agency*.

TEARS FALL ON ORKNEY

Nancy Saunders

TEARS FALL ON ORKNEY

ॐ

Nancy Saunders

Dear Jane. I'm on my way to Orkney. At last! I hope you don't mind first name terms. 'Miss Austen' sounds too distant and, even though we are separated by two centuries, I feel you are the one person who will understand where I'm coming from. Love. Isn't that the biggest question of all? I've stumbled from lover to lover with the thirst of someone lost in the desert. For the last two months I've thought of nothing but being here in Kirkwall – with Aidan. I have roughly known him for two years. He has brown eyes, sings songs about picking blackberries and can find a joke in anything. He bakes cupcakes filled with apple pieces and cinnamon, and walks everywhere. The last time I saw him he put new strings on my guitar.

I'm travelling all this way, chasing love. Imagine a great mechanical bird, big enough to hold one hundred people, and then picture it 20,000 feet high, flying above the clouds. We chase all over the world like this, in a matter of hours. There's still enough looking-out–of-the-window time, which I'm sure you will agree is an essential travelling companion. From my tiny window on the plane to Orkney I can see the hills around Edinburgh lie snug under a blanket of faded green velvet, and the snow on top of the

Cairngorms, like gentle spills of cream. From 16,000 feet, the string of islands looks like tiny, far away worlds. When we come down to land all I can see is the sea and then some grass and then we're bumping along the ground.

I know what you must be thinking. I admire Aidan, and yes – I think I have begun to love him. I've pictured us getting married and having a child and we're living in a cottage by the sea, growing vegetables. This is all quite hazy and only gazed at in the fleetest of moments. The pursuit of love is the one activity where I have boundless foolishness and daring.

Aidan meets me at the tiny airport and hugs me tight. We grin at each other like excited children. Then we drive to the sea. I have to change my shoes and while I'm lacing up my boots the clips I'd carefully put in my hair at 6 a.m. blow out in the wind. Aidan doesn't seem to notice. We charge off down the path and through a gate that Aidan points out isn't of the kissing sort; and then we run down to the beach. I find four stones marked with circles. Aidan does this thing where he picks up a stone to show me and as soon as I say, 'Oh that's nice,' he throws it into the sea! He's so funny. I can hardly keep up with him; he springs up the rocks like a goat. We share the last three pieces of my Cadbury's Caramel – chocolate that ordinarily I would eat all myself. It's the strangest feeling flying into the moment I've been thinking about for so long.

We run back along the path, pushing each other towards puddles. This is a basic form of what you called the Art of Flirting, I think. As we stand on top of the cliff catching our breath, Aidan says he would like to take some time out to do his music while I'm here, which I say is absolutely fine, even though my heart drops like a stone. We drive to Kirkwall, the main town hunkered down in the bay, the houses and buildings clinging together like barnacles. We have a lunch of chicken and coriander soup that Aidan has made then we walk into town to the museum. It's about to close so we pass all the glass cabinets filled with artefacts and have a go at building the model of the cathedral made out of colour-coded blocks to show when each bit had been added. We make our own design with a red turret, a blue east wing and an orange vestry.

Afterwards we go to Tesco's. There are no small shops anymore, only enormous buildings where you can buy everything. We mess about, talking loudly and laughing and Aidan knocks packets of spaghetti off the shelf. People frown at us as if we are drunk. Then Aidan stares at a pretty girl with dark hair. When we pass her a second time he stands transfixed. We walk back across the quay and he says that the girl was a runner-up in Miss Scotland. 'Really?' I say. 'I didn't notice.'

Aidan races up and down the stairs. All this rushing. He reminds me of Dustin Hoffman in *The Graduate*. It's the part when Dustin Hoffman is on a date with the girl he really likes, but he's charging off in front of her and she can hardly keep up. He leads her into a strip joint (where women dance around bare-breasted in a suggestive manner. You wouldn't believe it, but this was Women's Rights in the 20th century). Dustin Hoffman gawps at the naked women, and the expression of the girl shows her confusion and hurt. I should explain that we have things called Films. They are a little bit like looking at a mirror filled with the reflections of people acting out scenes, like in a play – but you can watch it all and it seems real. If only you could see your Mr Darcy, Jane. He's been in two film versions of *Pride and Prejudice*, and you'd be hard-pressed to choose between Colin Firth and Matthew Macfadyen. They're both dark eyed and smouldering.

*

It's the end of my first day. Aidan and I have just watched a film. We sat on the sofa together, me in the middle and Aidan leaning up against the far corner. The film claimed to be scary but it wasn't. There was a bit where the man and the woman got stuck in a passionate embrace, inside a ruined church deep in snow. When they started undoing each other's buttons I said to Aidan – things could get chilly. He sniffed, a sort of laugh but not laugh. When the film finished Aidan yawned. He's given up his bed (a double bed) for me, which is kind, and his towel too. I'm lying under his freshly washed sheets, all fired up. My heart is racing. When I saw myself in the mirror I had that sparkly-eyed look of someone who's falling for someone.

It's only the first night and I can't sleep. I think about when I last saw Aidan. He stayed with me for two nights. It was freezing and we walked for miles through the wood to reach the village pub. Over two pints Aidan told me of the time he nearly died but held on because his friend was there and he didn't want to let his friend down. We walked back through the wood after dark. The moon was full and its silver light gleamed off the naked trees. When we got home and warmed ourselves in front of the fire, all I could think about was covering Aidan's face with soft kisses. Instead I poked the logs in the fire. He reached out and touched my hair. We played roulette until we could play no more; then we said goodnight.

Wednesday. It doesn't look like it's raining but it is. We sit in the kitchen drinking Guatemalan coffee and watching the ferry push its way through the bay to Shapinsay. I imagine you did a great deal of tea drinking and looking out at the rain. Outside in the field a pattern of oystercatchers are digging for worms with their long, orange beaks. Aidan keeps singing the first line of 'Getting to know you'. We fall into one of our talks. Aidan likes to pull apart the reasoning of life, to show there's nothing holding it up but perception. He says he feels no desire, and asks me, 'What is a person?' I try to explain that we are driven beings with the need to make sense of the world and the people in it. He asks me, 'What is anger?' I try to explain about emotions, how necessary they are. I say that as far as *I* can see, his views are a form of defence. He says that if you stare at a single point for long enough, everything else in your vision blacks out.

We go for a walk in the rain, along a path that hugs the sea; our heads bent against the cold. The rocks are littered with plastic tubing and buoys washed up from the nearby fishery. As usual Aidan walks as if there's somewhere else he'd rather be. 'You have two modes,' I call out. 'The first is Aidan Jokey Mode, and the second, Aidan Words Mean Nothing.' He smiles, unsure. He asks me about the film we watched. He says there were a lot of flashbacks for such a simple story. I agree. The motivations of the characters were way too obvious. Aidan leads me to a bench facing out to sea. He shows me two names carved into the wood. 'Dan and Sophie; they came to stay. One evening they went out for a walk, sat on this bench. When they came back Sophie said Dan had asked her to marry him. She said yes.'
'How romantic.' I say. Then we turn and walk away.

We're sitting on the sofa in the sunny room with a view right across the bay, and our conversation accidentally touches on love. I ask Aidan, 'what are your pre-requisites?' He crosses his arms. 'I don't have any. Things just happen.' I want to remind him of the time he told me how a girl had broken his heart. I want to ask 'How can a man with no desire have his heart broken?'

When we pop in to see Aidan's brother and his wife, it's like the two of us dropping by. I watch Aidan while everyone is talking, and I am filled with that quiet, deep, heart-swelling sort of happiness. I stole the words right out of your mouth, but they fit so well, Jane, I couldn't help it. Aidan says he may get married one day and have children. He says it like he might pop out to the shops for a pint of milk.

Oh, Jane. What was it you said about the anxiety of expectation and the pain of disappointment? It's Friday night already and we're going to bed early (separately) to catch the small plane to North Ronaldsay first thing in the morning. It's a trip Aidan's organised for the weekend with a group of his friends – all women! He said it's not like their sex is relevant. I beg to differ. I'd like to see his face if I asked him to stay with four gorgeous blokes and me as the lucky girl. This trip will be a Test of Character type experience. To bed: enough of dreaming.

I knew it. The four women are beautiful. Not only that, they are French and German and Scottish, which means they speak with voices to melt any man. Their names are Odette and Silke, Ailean and Innes. While we're waiting for the plane they sit quietly, hardly speaking. I want to hate them and I almost do, but I can't because they are friendly which is worse, because I feel loathsome and want to crawl back under my stone. I can't help watching how Aidan is: whether he laughs longest with Innes, his gaze is deeper for Silke or his hand lingers on Ailean's arm. Between him and

Odette, something hangs unspoken. When we arrive the others squeeze around the tiny kitchen table in the hostel. I don my waterproof trousers and march off into the drizzle.

I am much calmed by my walk. I lean over a wall and watch the seals lounging about on the rocks. They lie with their backs against the cold, sharp edges, peering at me from upside down. They scratch and clap their feet, as if relaxing on chaise longues and deep-pile carpets. Mist floats down over the sea and I feel the peace that often comes with being alone.

Jane, this is not the first time I've fallen down the well of my own vanity. I've seen meaning in the few hopeful words Aidan has given me, words that could just as easily have been offered in friendship. It's like reaching the top of a mountain only to find that I'm the same person I was when I set out. It is the view that's changed. It's exhilarating; yet I feel like a small balloon not quite set free.

At dusk the six of us slip across rocks in the rain, clambering down to the beach. We watch the strange sight of sheep eating seaweed by the edge of the sea, their delicate legs like burnt matchsticks, lightly tripping over the rocks. We wait for each other as we clamber along. Perhaps we're each a little in love with Aidan. In the evening we eat pasta and drink wine and play charades, shrieking with laughter at each other's frantic mimes, our damp coats hanging over doors and our faces pink. What a desolate island this is; how spellbindingly beautiful.

In the morning the sun is soft and the sky an unblemished blue. We head out for a walk along the sandy beach stripped bare by the tide. We move along, sometimes together in pairs, sometimes scattered apart. Aidan runs up behind me and hurls us both towards the oncoming waves. He shows me an empty shell then hurls it out to sea. Then he picks up a small piece of wood smoothed into the shape of a wave. I wait for him to throw it away, but he gives it to me and I hold it in my hand. When he isn't looking I tuck it inside my pocket. On the way back we pass a field of lapwings dancing in the air. They suddenly drop and roll, their paddle-shaped wings flapping about drunkenly, then up again; their wheezing, bubbling song catching on the wind.

While I'm packing up my waterproofs, Aidan and Odette are covering each other in pretend punches and karate kicks. A little later Odette looks at me and says, 'you've caught the sun.'

My last day. I help Aidan strip the bed. He says if he washes everything now he can move back in to his room tonight. Jane, I'm one step closer to knowing myself. Love – if it does – shouldn't it just happen?

Aidan tells me of a time he flew away from Orkney. He says tears rolled down his face. He doesn't call it crying. He just says, 'The tears kept on falling.'

We say goodbye.

Later, flying away, I cry.

❧

My inspiration: I wanted to capture a little of Jane Austen's universal truths. Unrequited love seemed to be high on the list; it also has a timeless quality – an affliction human beings will continue to endure despite the world changing around them. Jane was also a prodigious letter writer – a format she perhaps considered a safe place in which to write down her true feelings. I wanted to mirror this in the style of the story. It was only when I finished writing that I realised my narrator had remained nameless. Perhaps the mark of a truly universal 'I'.

EIGHT YEARS LATER

Elaine Grotefeld

EIGHT YEARS LATER

❧

Elaine Grotefeld

They turned the corner and Chris *knew* this was the place, even before he saw the sign. He gripped the steering wheel to hide the onset of trembling.

Beside him his mother peered through her new-for-the-trip prescription sunglasses at the handsome red-brick house. 'We're here,' she cried, and slapped the dashboard.

He still hadn't told her.

There was nowhere to park directly outside the house – which he liked, it reminded him this wasn't North America – but they found a place down a leafy side street. His arm under hers, Chris led his mother towards the house. They passed an open area with a few swings – where a young boy and his dad (Chris presumed) rugby-tackled each other on to the long grass, rolled in the last warm days of summer. No sign of the mother... was she in the house? He both hoped – and hoped not.

He took in the large, square building set sideways to the road so that the white front door faced a green expanse of garden. He scanned the big Georgian windows on the ground floor.

'I wonder which one she sat by to write.' He tried to remember the snippets he'd once learnt about Jane Austen, this extraordinarily witty writer, favourite author of the two women he admired – and, yes, loved – most in all the world. One of them was Catherine, his mother, leaning on his arm now and quietly wheezing. She wore a pink summer hat and had brought a different one for each day. She didn't do bald well and wigs made her itch. He thought again of Ms Austen – hadn't she written the whole of *Persuasion* while she lived here – in a hurry, it was thought, already feeling ill?

Catherine squeezed his arm. 'Thank you for bringing me here, Chris,' she said. 'It's the best birthday present you could have ever given me.'

'You're only fifty once, Mom.'

'Thank God,' she said. 'I don't think much of it so far – apart from this trip, of course. I have much higher hopes for sixty and seventy.'

He smiled but his eyes stung. They both knew she'd be lucky to reach fifty-one.

Time to confess. He turned to face her, placed his hands on her shoulders, felt her bones through her shirt.

'Mom,' he said. 'There's something I need to tell you before we go in. I should have told you before but didn't know how. Can we stroll round the garden a bit first?'

She tilted her head back to study his face. 'I thought there was something,' she said. 'Lead on.'

Five minutes later, they stood together at the white front door, a little giddy from the scent of mint and roses – and their conversation.

'We're still early,' Catherine said. 'She won't be here for a while.' She sounded preoccupied – no wonder – it had been a lot for her to take in. And for Chris to explain – to compress eight years of intense and private longing into the five minutes it took to tell all. He'd tried to make his mother understand that the Jane Austen pilgrimage to England (they'd been to Bath first), and the visit to Oxford, Catherine's hometown, was all about *her*, about him and her sharing the adventure. The other idea had come later.

Chris bent to get through the doorway and led Catherine into a small entrance room, where they were greeted by a smiling lady about his mother's age. A collection of Jane Austen postcards, pens and notebooks lay on a few wooden tables and shelves but the commercialisation of Jane was *nothing* by American standards – much to Chris's relief.

'Thank you,' said Chris, admiring the gleaming wooden floor, the light through the window, the painted white shutters. 'We're delighted to be here.'

'Oh' said the lady, eyes bright with interest. 'Where are you from?'

'Well,' Chris began. 'I'm from Vancouver, Canada – but my mom here, Catherine, came from England originally.'

'Many years ago,' Catherine added. 'I went to Canada to visit a friend and never came back.'

Her lovely voice, still distinctively English after 30 years in Canada, had developed a raspy edge of late and Chris noticed she spoke less and less.

'I tried to beat the Canadian accent out of my son but to no avail,' she said. 'Peer pressure and all that – young people nowadays – what more can I say?'

Chris grinned. This was more like the old Catherine. 'Sorry to be such a disappointment to you, Mom.'

'If you've come all this way just to bring your mum to Chawton,' the lady said, 'you can't be all bad.'

Catherine winked at her. 'Oh – *I'm* not the only reason we're here.'

Chris winced. This was getting a little *too much* like the old Catherine. 'Shall we go look around?' he said. 'While we have time?'

The house felt smaller inside than out, but there was much to marvel at. A little wooden table, placed by a window in the parlour, was the highlight. A sign on it read *Do Not Touch*. But Catherine would never get another chance and so Chris held her hand and, while nobody was looking, brushed both their fingertips across an inch of the actual surface Jane Austen must have touched herself. His hand tingled violently but perhaps it was nerves.

Next they inspected a display of family letters painstakingly written with quill and ink. When was the last time he'd actually *written* anything? Email had all but wiped out the personal letter. Even his undeniably romantic plea had been typed. Typed!

Catherine lingered over the letters, and Chris left her to it. Such a gift to see her *wrapt withal*. He wandered through or peeked into the small rooms alone, bending under the low door frames, inhaling the comforting smell of wood and ancient wallpaper. The floorboards creaked and squeezing himself down the narrow staircase he felt huge, like a bear, over-sized and clumsy amongst all these dainty artefacts and impossibly tiny period clothes.

He checked his watch. It was time. It felt like he'd just been whacked with a baseball bat in the back of the knees.

So many unknowns: would she have seen his notice in those Jane Austen online newsletters? And if she had, would she come? And if she came – would she still be *free*? He hadn't thought further than that.

Back downstairs, he heard his mother back in the front entry room.

'The thing is,' she was saying, 'my son has a deep, dark secret.'
'Oh?'
'Yes – he loves Jane Austen! He was always a great reader. I think he read his first when he was about fourteen. We were on some camping trip in the rain and he'd read everything including the camping stove instruction manual – excuse me, it's just a cough – anyway, he got so desperate he picked up my copy of *Persuasion*. He was so embarrassed to be found reading it, poor boy.'

Persuasion. Where his story had started.

Chris, aged seventeen, usually ran straight past the glass-fronted Starbucks on his way to the trail path through the woods, but that morning in late August, something – or rather someone – made him stop and stare inside.

A *person* – no longer a girl but hardly old enough to be called a woman – sat curled in the big armchair in the corner, wearing a simple white summer dress – and reading *Persuasion*. She even looked like the writer – petite, intelligent, impish. Prettier, though – but didn't everyone say that the one surviving likeness of Jane Austen didn't do her justice? Maybe this was how she'd *really* looked.

His heart rate spiked and he'd hardly started his run. *Chris is rather timid*, they said in his school reports, like it was a sin. He stared inside, wanted so much to go in, to go up and talk to her, maybe ask her about the book. He'd read it too, hadn't he? And loved it. *She* wouldn't find that odd. Surely.

But he didn't. He was too scared. He took one last look and pounded along the sidewalk towards the woods.

By the time he started back at school the following month he must have wandered into Starbucks about twenty times in the hope of seeing the girl again. He carried *Persuasion* in his backpack and was all set with his master plan to sit himself near her and 'coincidentally' produce the same book as hers. But she never showed – he'd blown his chance.

'We'd like you all to welcome our new English teacher,' the principal announced at the first assembly in September. 'Miss Anderson.'

And there she was – the girl from the coffee shop. She looked 19, but she had to be 23 – minimum. And she was his English teacher.

Obviously, he told himself to *forget it.*

But never had he looked forward to a class so much – and never had he wanted more for time to slow down during it. Miss Jean Anderson was sweet and clever and funny and spoke with a soft English accent. Like Jane Austen – whom she adored. She wore summer dresses at first, and then in fall exchanged them for long wool skirts and lace-up boots, and a purple velvet cloak that was totally impractical in the Vancouver rain but he loved to see her in it. He feared others would mock her for her eccentricity but nobody did. She was *English*, after all, only been in Canada since college, so that seemed to explain it. Everybody loved her.

As did he. But differently from the rest. She was six years his senior and his *teacher,* and to make any kind of approach to her seemed to him to be not just preposterous and out of the question, but to be a gross imposition on her sweetness, her sunny innocence.

But he couldn't hide his feelings altogether. He sought extra 'help', would 'swing by' her classroom during breaks to 'ask her advice' about whatever project was in play. He even got Catherine to invite her over for dinner since they were both such ardent admirers of Jane Austen. The more he saw of her the more he loved her – but she never so much as held his gaze.

Until that evening in May, when she'd let him walk her home.
You pierce my soul.

She left at the end of the school year. Not just the school, but the
country. Everyone was shocked. She had only just arrived, she was
such a wonderful teacher – why would she leave so soon?

Only Chris understood. If she'd stayed, *something would have
happened*. They'd *acknowledged* their attraction with their eyes;
that was all. But Chris felt it, heard it, like a hum in the air. Perhaps
she did too. In any case, to his modern-day Jane, the territory was
too dangerous.

There were other girls, of course – but none to compare. He
always thought of her. Furtively he'd read the novels of Jane
Austen over and over because they made him feel *connected* to
Miss Jean Anderson. He could hear her voice when he read, could
even catch her trademark lavender scent. Chris was a romantic
who badly wanted to find his *true love*. But knew in his heart he'd
already met her – his very own Anne Elliot – only he didn't know
how to find her again.

Chris and his mother were back in the front room – having
revisited the garden, examined the donkey carriage, reread every
letter. Always listening for the sound of new footsteps.

It was eight years since he'd last seen her, and one hour and
eight minutes past *the time*. Miss Anderson wasn't coming.

'Are you ready to go, Mom?' Chris said gently.

His mother hesitated. 'I was so sure she would come – it's very
odd.' She glanced once more at the clock. 'Do you mind if I get
some postcards, dear?'

She took a while choosing and the lady behind the counter
glanced at her watch and kept glancing at the door as if wanting to
lock up. After Chris paid for the postcards (he insisted), the woman

said, 'It's closing soon, but you've just time to visit Chawton House too while you're here.' She paused. 'It's just down the road and the library is superb.'

Chris dropped his change on the floor.

'*Chawton House*?' he said. 'I thought this was Chawton House?'

'Oh no, dear, this is just the cottage belonging to the estate. This is Jane Austen's house, yes, but Chawton House is the grand Elizabethan mansion where her brother—'

'I told her the wrong place,' he told his mother, already pulling her towards the door. 'I can't believe it.'

'It's straight down that road,' said the lady, in the doorway now. 'On your left – you can't miss it.'

Chris just about dragged his poor mother back to the car and they sped off towards the real Chawton House, turned into a classic long driveway with the mansion standing proud and imposing at the other end. It was 4.50 p.m. and it closed in ten minutes. Would she even be there?

A bright red mini came speeding along the driveway towards them. Chris caught a glimpse of the driver as she passed – and did a hand brake turn.

They found the mini in their old parking spot.

Thank you God, Chris thought as, once again, he led his mother – more urgently this time – back into Jane Austen's house.

He found Miss Jean Anderson in the entry room. She turned as they came in – and her smile, after eight long years, re-booted his heart.

'You read my posting,' he said.

She nodded. 'Yes – I'd give it an A for resourcefulness... but a D for research.'

He grinned. 'I know – I got the house wrong. But look – we're both here now, aren't we?'

'So *you're* the young man with the message!' exclaimed the lady. 'I had a feeling it was you.'

'So you suggested we go to Chawton House?' Chris said. 'Just in case?'

She winked. 'Being here all the time, Jane's genius can't help but rub off a little, you know.'

He looked with love on these three extraordinary women – and had an overwhelming sense of there being *four* people in the room with him.

'Maybe it's being in Jane Austen's house,' he said, 'but I have the oddest sensation—'

'The end of *Persuasion*, right?' Jean said. 'You feel like we're in it?'

'I need to check the rooms before closing up,' the lady said to Catherine – 'would you care to join me?' They both withdrew.

Chris stepped forward, took Jean's hand. Her cool palm pressed against his... no rings. He'd found her. He was 25 now, she was 31. She was probably still an English teacher – but not *his*. He *loved* her. So far so good – on his side.

But what about *hers?*

He took a deep breath. '*I am half agony, half hope.*'

She smiled. 'You're late,' she said. 'But not *too* late.'

❧

My inspiration: In Jane Austen's *Persuasion* I love the idea of finding again a love you thought was lost and wanted to recreate Captain Wentworth's 'half agony, half hope' in a modern context. Captain Wentworth and his impassioned letter to Anne inspired the idea of a male viewpoint in my story. I also thought it would be fun to base the action at Jane Austen's house in Chawton – albeit not Chawton House itself.

BROKEN WORDS

Suzy Ceulan Hughes

BROKEN WORDS

❧

Suzy Ceulan Hughes

'So, how are things?' he said.

She held the lead rope loosely in one hand and scurried the fingers of the other through the pony's mane. As he lifted a foot to remove the old shoe, the pony leant into her and rested its muzzle against her arm.

'Life is good,' she said. 'Though I'm not sleeping very well.'

At night, in the long hours, she was beset by ghosts and poisonous regrets. Why are they called the small hours, she thought, when they are so very long? To sleep, she had to turn her back to the north, to feel the weight of the mountain behind her, protecting her.

'Have you tried counting sheep?' he said.

She gazed across the fields to the ridge of hills on the north side of the Dyfi. In the foreground, the grass dazzled green in the sunlight, polka-dotted white with sheep.

'No,' she said. 'I can't bear them. I've tried counting stars, but there are too many of them and I soon give up.'

Her mother used to talk about stars. 'You should count your lucky stars. Wish upon a falling star and your dreams will come true. It's all in the stars.' The star sayings went along with others. 'You've made your bed, so you must lie in it. You can't have your cake and eat it. When your time is up...' It all made life seem rather hopeless. As though you occasionally had the power to choose and create bad things for yourself, but never anything good.

Frost was lying in shaded pockets and on north-facing slopes. The pony's feet steamed and its breath hovered in the air. In the village, smoke from the chimneys hung heavily, drifting in curling waves over the rooftops.

'Perhaps I'll try counting waves,' she said. 'I've always loved sleeping on boats, though it's something I haven't done for years.'

Her father had had a boat. He had always had boats but, for a while, he had one with a proper cabin and sleeping berths. They would sail out to the islands and moor up for the night off one of the beaches. She had loved to swim in the ink-black sea, to watch the phosphorescence play around her barely visible legs. Her father never swam at night. He said somebody had to stay on board just in case. She had sometimes wondered about that. Just in case of what? At the time, it had never crossed her mind that it might be dangerous. To swim at night, out there.

'I'm not sure I'd fancy that,' he said.

He stood at the pony's left shoulder, his back towards its head, and bent over to lift its left foot and slip it between his legs, so that the back of the pony's knee rested against the back of his, and its foot was cradled in his hand. The clipped horn fell to the ground like crescent moons.

A dozen seagulls had joined the polka-dot sheep, skimming low, strutting their stuff on the green baize, searching for food. Perhaps there was a storm out at sea. Wasn't that what they said? That seagulls inland meant bad weather at sea?

Her parents had inhabited polarised worlds. All air and water, she thought. Not a scrap of solid ground between them. Even their languages were not translatable from one to the other. It was a simple question of semantics. Neither of them had any vocabulary for taking responsibility. So, she'd had to find her own piece of solid ground, her own shoes to walk away in.

'I'll put new shoes on the front,' he said. 'The hind ones can go back on this time.'

The small furnace roared in the back of the van. The red-hot shoes would hiss with seeming fury when they were plunged in water. A cloud of steam would rise and disperse. This much she knew.

She and her parents had stopped speaking. It was for the best. Her new language had words with meanings that simply could not exist in theirs, like love and solid and rock. She had her own clichés now. The man she loved was as solid as a rock. He had once wondered, out loud, who would look after her if something happened to him. "Who would look after you if something happened to me?" he had said. She had supposed she would look after herself.

Again, he drew the pony's leg between his thighs and placed the shoe. He held the nails between his lips, taking each one as he needed it. They had flat, rectangular heads, and the shaft tapered to a fine point.

'Do you know the story,' she said, 'of the Black Bull of Norroway?'

He hammered a nail into place and glanced up at her, sideways, with two nails still held softly between his lips. He paused before answering her, pinching the nails between the thumb and index finger of his left hand and holding them away from his mouth so he could speak.

'I don't know that I do,' he said. 'But if you tell me what it's about, perhaps I'll recognise it, all the same.'

'It's about a young woman who, by her own small error, finds herself abandoned in the Valley of Glass. The floor and walls of the valley are all made of glass, and the more she tries to scramble up the sides, the more she slides back. In the end, she can do nothing but crawl on her hands and knees around the edge of the valley, looking for a way out.

'Just as she is about to give up, to curl up and wait for death to come to her, she finds a blacksmith's forge tucked deep into the side of the valley. The blacksmith – he can be young and handsome or old and gnarled, whichever you wish – listens to her story and takes pity on her. He promises to make her a pair of iron shoes to help her climb out of the valley, but first she must work for him for seven years without complaining.

'And so the young woman – she can be any age you please, really – pumps the bellows and holds the tongs and passes the blacksmith his tools for seven long years without once complaining, though it is hard and heavy work, and the heat from the furnace scalds her skin red and raw.

'Finally, at the end of the seven years, the blacksmith thanks her for her work and makes her a pair of iron shoes whose soles are set with spikes. But he knows no way of fastening them other than to nail them to her feet, which is what he does.

'Of course, the young woman is in agony, and every step she takes sends pain shivering through her body. But, as we already know, she is a stalwart soul and she clambers up the smooth side of the Valley of Glass until she reaches its rim and is free. The End.'

'You mean that after all that she doesn't even get to marry a prince?'

'Well, of course she does, but it's a long story and I've told you the interesting bit.'

'I see,' he said. 'But I'd like to hear the ending, nonetheless.'

He drew the pony's leg forwards and upwards, placing its foot on the metal tripod. He clenched the tips of the nails and rasped them smooth and safe. Like a manicurist, he filed the edges of the hoof tight to the shoe, sending slivers of horn falling to the ground.

'There,' he said. 'All done.'

She slipped the head collar from the pony's head and they sat on the top bar of the gate to watch as the pony went back out into the field. It moved slowly at first, as though getting the feel of its new shoes. Then it dipped and tossed its head – like a ballerina, she thought – before arching its neck and trotting away towards the herd, its steps slow and elevated and its tail raised like a fine plume behind it.

He turned to her and smiled. 'So,' he said, 'she marries the prince in the end. But how did she come to be in the Valley of Glass? What was her own small error? And who is the Black Bull of Norroway?'

She stared at him. 'So many questions,' she said. 'And I am not Scheherazade.'

He jumped down from the gate. 'I'm sorry,' he said. 'I just—'

She watched him as he wiped his hands against his leather chaps and gathered his tools, ready for the next pony. He was a very kind young man, she thought. Perhaps there was something about him that reminded her. Perhaps that was why she had started to tell him the story. She had lied about the prince. And the beginning of the story had never been told.

In the beginning, she had felt as though she had been saved from herself, though she had not understood quite what she meant by that, at the time. He had been tall and strong and big of bone and heart. She had felt safe. She had imagined she might be looked after for the first time. For the first time, she had imagined she might be looked after. But he had gone away and he had not come back, though she had waited and waited and waited.

'The girl and the bull,' she said, 'are travelling together. At first, she is uncertain of him and has no idea of their destination. But he carries her gently and safely, and she finds that she can lean against his great, black shoulders without fear.

'They have been travelling some time together in this way, in quiet companionship, when they come to a dark valley overhung with brooding cliffs. This is the Valley of Glass and the Black Bull of Norroway must fight its guardian if they are to pass through safely.

'"Sit on this rock," the bull tells her. "If the sky turns blue and the sun begins to shine, you'll know the battle is won. But should everything turn red, you'll know I've lost. Above all, don't move. If you so much as wriggle your toes, I'll never be able to find you again."

'So the girl sits on the rock and waits. And when the sky turns blue and the sun begins to shine, bathing the valley around her in blue-gold light, she smiles. She watches as the bull comes ambling back towards her, his broad shoulders flecked with blood. But he cannot see her. She calls to him, but he does not hear. And he never sees or speaks to her again, although she sees and speaks to him all the time.'

There was a long silence between them. The ponies had settled to grazing beneath the line of oak trees that ran across the centre of the field. A chaffinch hopped around the edges of the manure pile, seeking delicacies. Traffic hummed on the main road through the village.

'So her one small error wasn't an error at all,' he said.

'No,' she said. 'She didn't do anything wrong. But she broke the spell that joined their worlds. The door was still there, but it had been closed on her. And even if she had been able to open it, perhaps she would have found nothing on the other side.'

'Nothing?' he said.

'Oh, you know,' she said. 'Some doors are better left closed, and all that. You never know what you might find behind them. And nothing is always a possibility. A blank, impenetrable wall, perhaps. Sometimes it's better to leave the door closed than to contemplate what is, or might have been, behind it. The door might be very beautiful in itself. An ancient oak door, say, with a single extraordinary hinge. The hinge, of course, is not a hinge, any more than the door is a door. But it is also very beautiful. It is a hinge forged of horseshoes. You can see the curving shapes, the nail holes; the groove that provides the grip. The ends of the shoes are hammered into simple flowers, like daisies. The door goes nowhere. It does not open. The hinge serves no purpose. It is pure ornament. It is all a comforting deception.'

'Like the prince?' he said.

'Ah,' she said, 'the prince. I suppose I must tell you that the girl has rather cannily held on to three magic fruits, each of which she has been instructed to cut when she meets the first great need of her life. I never fail to wonder why she doesn't cut at least one of them to avoid those seven years of mourning in the Valley of Glass, or at the very least to avoid the agony of that hideous shoeing of iron. But she's right, you know, because in the end she needs all three of those magic fruits to conquer the demons who would see her finally vanquished and to secure her love.'

'Hmm,' he said.

'Well, precisely,' she said. 'I did say I'd told you the interesting bit. Shall we get this last pony's feet trimmed? At least this one doesn't wear shoes.'

She held the lead rope, standing first on one side of the pony's head, and then on the other, and then back again, depending on which foot he was working on. It was a dance, choreographed over time, and the three of them knew the pattern of the steps and their pacing. They did not falter.

❧

I should like to acknowledge Kenneth McLeish's superb version of 'The Black Bull of Norroway' in *Tales of Wonder and Magic* by Berlie Doherty (ed).

❧

My inspiration: In February 2009 I was one of the lucky few to get through the snow to Chawton House to attend a writing workshop. There I found my horseshoe motif in the single hinge on the ancient oak door set against a wall in the Long Gallery. Jane Austen's life and work provided my central theme: sometimes through our own choice or error, sometimes because of external events and circumstances, doors close on relationships. In life, they might never again open, even if we wish them to; in fiction we might hope for redemption in a prince or a Mr Darcy.

MISS AUSTEN VICTORIOUS

Esther Bellamy

MISS AUSTEN VICTORIOUS

Esther Bellamy

'It is a truth universally acknowledged that a single man in possession of a good fortune must be in want of a wife,' Mrs Bennet announced.

Mr Bennet, wedged between the wings of a Sheraton armchair, lowered his newspaper, which bore the headlines '72 killed in V2 rocket attack', and inquired cautiously over the top of it, 'Is that his design in settling here?'

Mrs Bennet nodded vigorous encouragement in his direction, before throwing back her head and hands in order to signal exasperation.

'You take delight in vexing me; you have no compassion on my nerves.'

Mr Bennet gave a sort of bleat and peered frantically at Miss Bates, who was squeezed uncomfortably behind the curtain on a camp stool, but whilst trying to find her place in the script she had dropped her spectacles and, whilst groping for them frantically, she was unaware of the emanations of distress from the armchair, or indeed of anything else.

Mrs Bennet, almost equally unaware, blundered on. 'Ah you do not know what I suffer—' She stopped abruptly as it finally occurred to her that she had not given Mr Bennet the chance to make her suffer. He had not refused to wait upon Mr Bingley and, mouth half open from anxiety, showed not the faintest signs of doing so. Mrs Bennet leapt in to the breach and extemporised furiously.' 'Since you have already said that you will not visit Mr Bingley what use is it if twenty such men visit the neighbourhood?'

Inspiration came to Mr Bennet and he assured Mrs Bennet with the glee of a man who sees the end of a scene in sight, 'depend upon it, my dear, when there are twenty I shall visit them all.'

They stared at each other in delight at their mutual cleverness. Lady Baverstoke, realising that the scene was over, clapped.

Mrs Bennet turned to her husband also clapping, 'Oh well done, Gerald! Well done! You see, I told you you would remember the lines on the night.'

Mr Bennet muttered something about its only being the dress rehearsal.

Polly, relentlessly modern in trousers, despite Lady Baverstoke's protests, trudged onto the set and began moving the furniture back for the ball at Netherfield. Mr Bingley, aged not quite seventeen, trailed after her, transfixed by the uniform trousers. She completely ignored him. Mr Bennet was chivvied out of his armchair and it was pushed to the side.

'Are the girls ready?' Mrs Bennet asked Polly. She did not bother to lower her voice being rather keen to emphasise her role as actor and director to Lady Baverstoke.

'You've got them all except a Mary,' replied Polly.

'Oh really! She absolutely *promised* me to be here on time tonight.'

'Well she's not going to be here at all. One of the chaps she does fire-watch duty with is ill, so Muriel said she'd stand in tonight. She asked me to tell you but I didn't get a chance before. She said she was sure you would understand.'

That was not quite true.

'Really it's too bad, the dress rehearsal, I do think Muriel could have made the effort.'

Polly attempted to be conciliatory.

'Well Mary doesn't say much does she? She just has to look disapproving most of the time.'

'But the piano! Muriel's the only one who can play the piano.'

'I could play the piano if you like, Emma,' interjected Lady Baverstoke, 'I know the music and,' coyly, 'I certainly know the piano.'

Mrs Bennet looked put out but while she felt that it was very much her play and her cast she could hardly deny that it was Lady Baverstoke's double drawing room and Lady Baverstoke's piano. It had also been Lady Baverstoke's idea to put on a play 'for the war effort.'

Lady Baverstoke's house, and double drawing room in particular, had had a very quiet war and, despite a front of magnificent indifference, she was not deaf to acid comments from the WVS and others of that ilk. Baverstoke Park was housing the contents of an important portrait gallery, rather than evacuees, for the duration. On the whole Lady Baverstoke considered the portraits a wonderful addition to the house; in the drawing room an eighteenth-century lady in yellow now went beautifully with the watered-silk curtains. By this ruse, acres of carpet, yards of curtains and masses of furniture remained jealously protected from hoi poloi by her ladyship. She spoke vaguely of 'preserving standards' and shook her head with regretful decision when asked if she had any material to donate for the making of clothes for bombed-out families.

Lady Baverstoke had spent England's Finest Hour stockpiling sufficient sugar and sherry to last a thousand years. By The End of the Beginning she was the dedicated enemy of the ARP, the WVS and the Captain of the local Home Guard, to that list she could now add GIs. However, it seemed that the Americans were shortly to be foisted on the deserving French and Lady Baverstoke, sugar and sherry supplies still holding out, felt quite able to do a little fundraising in aid of the victory that must surely be at hand. Putting on a play had struck her as a means of putting her drawing room to a use that was both patriotic and elegant. Surprisingly she had found a ferocious ally in the vicar's wife, Mrs Emma Houghton. No one could have accused Mrs Houghton of having a quiet war. She had billeted evacuees, rolled bandages, knitted balaclavas and had sent exhausted survivors of Dunkirk on their way armed with strong tea and tart jam sandwiches. And she sat on committees.

That Lady Baverstoke had never sat on a committee with Mrs Houghton before was proof of her powerful, if latent, political instinct. Furthermore, realising that it is much easier to steer a committee from below than to order it from above, she had helped elect Mrs Houghton to be president of the newly formed Amateur Dramatics Committee.

Something very English, the committee felt, would be desirable in the circumstances. Someone promptly suggested Shakespeare. Someone else, perhaps not without a touch of malice, suggested *Henry V* and the possibility of involving local evacuees. Lady Baverstoke was not the only person with visions of these willing little extras re-enacting the battle of Agincourt through her drawing room. Some kind soul pointed out that the imminent film, with its rather superior resources made a play rather unnecessary just now. No one could remember just who it had been who suggested Jane Austen but everyone, without quite explaining how, felt that she struck the right note; highbrow but not too difficult to understand, obviously. Very English, of course, and perfect for acting in a large drawing room.

Getting enough men for the play had been a problem; nothing but Christian fortitude, patriotic duty and fear of his wife would have made the Reverend Gerald Houghton take to the stage as Mr Bennet. He could now be observed getting in to character for the Netherfield ball scene by showing the greatest possible reluctance. His wife's glance swept proprietarily over the cast as the Bennet girls trooped in.

'Lizzy!' admonished Mrs Bennet, 'wipe that lipstick off. It's far too bright anyway, not right for the period at all.'

'Mrs Houghton's quite right, dear,' urged Lady Baverstoke.

'But we'll look such frights,' protested Lizzy. 'We're all wearing modern evening dresses and you can't then say that everything else has to be Regency, it doesn't make sense.' She rolled her eyes and gave her mouth a desultory wipe. 'There, will that do?'

'For now,' agreed Mrs Bennet. Now line up for the dance; chaps on one side...oh dear, oh dear we do need more *men.'*

'There'll be two more on the night,' pointed out Polly, 'me and Rosalind—'

'Rosalind and I, dear,' interposed Lady Baverstoke.

'Rosalind and I in our hunting kit. The others will just have to dance with each other.'

'Polly will you dance now?'

'All right, come on, Alice.' Alice bounced forward but Mrs Bennet swooped.

'No, no, Alice must dance with Mr Bingley. It says so in the book. He dances first with Charlotte Lucas. Come along Henry.' (Mr Bingley was her nephew.) He shuffled forward. Charlotte and

Mr Bingley, being sixteen and seventeen respectively, turned scarlet. They were hustled to the front of the stage, touching each other only when and where strictly necessary.

'Now is everyone ready?' A figure drifted to the edge of the stage with an expression of nervous inquiry. 'No, Mr Darcy, off stage, we don't need you yet, not until your grand entrance.' The figure vanished with alacrity.

'Now,' to Lady Baverstoke, 'could we have a waltz please? We begin the dancing and Mr Darcy comes in.'

Lady Baverstoke smiled and obliged, with the 'Blue Danube'. To Mrs Bennet's irritation she was very good but in her role as director she had more pressing concerns. After a few bars she began to glare towards the wings. The second time she waltzed past she risked a gesticulation and Mr Darcy, accompanied by Miss Bingley, moved to the centre of the stage with the high-shouldered, stork-legged gait of a man who fears that his breeches are going to fall down. He had been outvoted by the females of the cast who were quite determined that Mr Darcy should wear breeches. (Mr Bingley was luckier; simply appearing in his Eton tails which had been deemed quite suitable.) Lady Baverstoke had donated her late husband's court dress but the late Lord Baverstoke had been cheerfully corpulent and the current Mr Darcy was not. Despite belt and braces, he was in miseries.

The casting of Ken Thornton as Mr Darcy had been a worry to Lady Baverstoke, of course he was terribly good-looking and he sounded alright, more or less, but her nephew Reggie had sniggered dreadfully when she told him.

'Good Lord, you mean you're casting a Brylcreem boy as the quintessential English hero?'

'Well, my dear, what else can I do? You wouldn't care to play the part I suppose?'

'No fear. I'll probably be in France by then anyway. And I think I'd rather be there,' he added with a laugh.

Whether Ken Thornton would rather have repeated a botched parachute landing somewhere over Beachy Head, which left him with three broken ribs and a few weeks leave, was a moot point. Certainly nothing but his being grotesquely in love with Emily Lowe, who was playing Lydia Bennet, would have induced him to spend the last of that leave cooped up in Lady Baverstoke's drawing room. Lydia had kissed him twice behind the scenes and promised to write to him. (She had also promised to write to one Coldstream guardsman, a Lieutenant in the Royal Hampshires and a Free French pilot. Her handwriting was not very clear.)

The dancers stopped and everyone stared at Ken. He really did look rather good in court dress. Mrs Bennet bore down on him and curtseyed. Mr Darcy bowed stiffly.

'There's nothing like dancing, sir, one of the refinements of polished society,' she opined.

'Every savage can dance,' Mr Darcy snapped.

He had actually forgotten the rest of the line and was trying to act but it sounded like truculent rudeness and not only Mrs Bennet but also Emma Houghton took it as such. She considered Ken Thornton's manner 'distinctly offhand'. She was annoyed by Polly's presence and Muriel's absence. She sensed that her cast did not really consider this play, her play, important, although her potent combination of cajolery and bullying had already sold out both performances. (Her cast had nearly rebelled about that second performance.) Nearly one hundred people at a shilling apiece, would be squeezed in to the drawing room to suffer the particular martyrdom offered by the church hall's folding chairs. Two performances would raise nearly ten pounds, which, Mrs Bennet considered, was quite a lot of spitfire for one village. She was tired, having spent all afternoon rehearsing, all morning volunteering at the nearest hospital and a fair portion of the night before sewing up the back of Jane Bennet's evening dress, which its occupant had managed to split from stem to stern at a party. Mrs Bennet felt that it was very unfair. At the end of the scene she sat back in the armchair, and eyed the other cast members with intent. They drew together instinctively.

'I don't know what is wrong with you children,' she began peevishly. 'All you do is complain—'

But Mrs Bennet was suddenly silent. The cast froze in a tableau around her chair. Lady Baverstoke, still at the piano stool, put her hand to her mouth as if to silence the tiny 'oh!' that escaped it. Slowly every face turned upward.

In another time and place, it is possible to think of a sound like a giant hornet's thrum, or perhaps the metallic burble of a motorbike passing down the lane. However, none of the people in that room had the luxury of metaphor or distance: instant terror bought instant recognition.

The engine of the V2 rocket chugged on, on, on.

Silence.

One or two people put their hands over their heads, but mostly they stared at the ceiling, the beautiful Angelica Kauffmann ceiling that, for a petrified moment, turned into a fabulous mosaic, before the cracks turned to raining plaster, the delicate carvings to relentless missiles. As everything that was solid and heavy in the world began falling—

They pulled Mrs Bennet out first, protesting furiously that they should have taken her nephew before her. Gradually the rest of the cast was disinterred, scratched and bruised but, with the exception of Mr Darcy's broken arm, essentially undamaged. The chief fireman came over as the survivors were being solicitously wrapped in blankets. Someone had managed the English conjuring trick of hot sweet tea for emergencies.

The officer surveyed them. 'You were lucky.'

Lady Baverstoke turned from surveying a house that had not a window left in it with wobbling lip and welling eye. She said, 'lucky?'

'If that had hit the house you'd all have been killed. As it was—' He indicated the crater that had once been a croquet lawn. 'You'd probably have been all right if it hadn't been for that rotten old ceiling.' It was too much for Lady Baverstoke who broke down again. The cast tried to comfort her but the fact remained that her drawing room was ruined and the rest of her house not much better. She was quite inconsolable and perhaps it was a little tactless of Mrs Bennet to declare, after a few more minutes, 'well, we'll simply have to move the play to the church hall.'

The cast gaped. Even Lady Baverstoke was silenced. Then Mr Darcy smiled at Mrs Bennet. 'Maybe a sling will improve my performance.'

Mrs Bennet turned on him a face like the rising sun.

'Oh, Ken, how noble of you!' The smile vanished under a tide of relief. 'Thank goodness I didn't have time to bring those chairs over from the church hall.'

≈

My inspiration: A Jane Austen novel seems the antithesis of violent chaos, although these novels were written between the Terror and Waterloo. They appear to be concerned with a thin veneer of civilised behaviour among an exclusive minority yet they have survived and flourished among readerships very different from the ones for which they were written. Jane Austen has always been associated with the country house but has proved herself well able to survive and flourish in much tougher circumstances.

CLEVERCLOGS

Hilary Spiers

CLEVERCLOGS

❧

Hilary Spiers

Yesterday I read 27,373 words. Not counting rereading the cereal packet. It would have been more but Dad took my torch away last night so I had to kneel on my bed to try to read by the light of the street lamp outside, with my head poking through the curtains. That was hard work, because I had to keep listening out for Mum's footsteps on the stairs. She's really sneaky, taking her shoes off at the bottom and creeping up to catch me out. 'You'll go blind reading in the dark,' she says. Which is stupid because all you are doing when you're reading is using your eyes, just the same as if you were looking where you are going or shopping in the supermarket or enjoying the view. Anyway, I wouldn't have had to read the cereal packet if Dad hadn't said at breakfast, 'It's rude to read at the table,' and taken my book away. He's always doing that.

The book I'm reading at the moment (or was until Dad took it away from me) is *Sense and Sensibility* by Jane Austen. Granny lent it to me. Dad flicked through it and said to Mum, 'Should she be reading this?' like it was one of those fat books Mum reads on holiday that I'm not allowed to borrow. Mum shrugged and said, 'It's a classic,' so Dad just put it on the counter until I'd finished my muesli. I hate muesli; when I stay over at Gina's, she has those little packets with all the different cereals in them. Mum says they're bad for your teeth, but what I had for breakfast had 22g of sugar per 100g, so I don't think that's very healthy either.

I worked out the number of words I'd read by using a formula. My formula is one page equals 350 words. You times the number of pages by 350 to get the total, and then add all the other words you've read during the day. You can count adverts and things like menus, but not road signs or shop names that you pass every day, because they're not new. I read 60 pages of *Sense and Sensibility* today, so that makes 21,000 words already. Then I added all the words in lessons (in books and on the board) and the hymns in assembly. Plus the torn bit of newspaper someone had left on the seat by the bus stop. And it came to 27,373.

I overheard Uncle Terry say to Mum once, 'She's a right little bookworm', like it was something not quite right. I looked it up. The dictionary said *Bookworm: An organism, sometimes a literal worm, which harms books by feeding on their binding or leaves. Also a term for a person devoted to books.* I think he meant the 'also' bit. I like the word devoted. It makes me think of *Little Women.* I've read that too.

I *yearn* to get back to Elinor and Marianne. Yearn is my word of the day. It means to long or ache or hanker for. I don't like hanker much because it sounds too close to handkerchief which is not serious enough. Granny gave me a very old dictionary, which looks like someone has picked at the cover with their nails. I think it might be covered in leather because it smells a bit funny and the pages are blobby with little brown marks. I looked up yearn in that and it said: *To have a strong, often melancholy desire.* And I thought that suited *Sense and Sensibility* because that is how I feel about it. It makes me scrunch my toes up and hold my breath. I've just read the bit where Marianne falls ill because of the horrible Willoughby, which was so terrible I could hardly bear it (even though I think Marianne is a bit of an idiot sometimes) and I wanted it to go on forever at the same time. This is why it is such a good book, because it's almost making you read it whether you want to or not.

Sometimes when I'm lying in bed at night, all the characters of all of the books I've read swim round my head in a mad dance. My head feels like it might burst with words sometimes and then I think that I've years and years of reading still to come and where do all the words go? Mrs Finch said in class that everything we ever see or do or read leaves a memory in our brains, but I've seen a picture of a brain and it's so *small*. And if we can't store all the words and stories, then how do we know we aren't just reading the same things over and over without knowing it? That's why I keep all the books I've read in my bedroom so I can prove to myself I know what they are about. Some of my friends test me sometimes, especially Harriet. She says, 'Okay, cleverclogs, tell me what happens in the book,' so I do. I tell her about all the characters and what happens to them and the sorts of things they say and how it makes me feel. I did that with *The Lord of the Rings*, but she said, 'Oh, I've seen that on DVD so I don't have to read it,' and even though I told her that the books were miles better and that the films left loads of stuff out, she didn't care. At first, Mrs Finch didn't believe I'd read all three books – it's called a trilogy – because she'd never met anyone as young as me who had. She didn't read them until she was at university. I told her I hope they have loads of books at university because I don't want to go there if it's full of things like *The Lord of the Rings* that I've already read. Although I wouldn't mind reading something like *Pride and Prejudice* again (but not straightaway), because there's so much going on and you can learn a lot about life in olden times. Plus Mrs Bennet is really funny.

Once I'd learnt what a bookworm was, the word kept coming up all over the place. It was in the paper yesterday morning in an article about Jacqueline Wilson and I saw it on the back of a book I picked up in the local bookshop on the way home from school. I didn't buy the book, I never do, unless it's my birthday or something, but I love being in there, surrounded by the smell of books. Sometimes I think words just hang around in the background waiting to be noticed and then when they are they get sort of brighter so they stand out. I don't like the 'worm' bit, but if that's what the word is, then I suppose I'm stuck with it. I wonder if there are jobs for people to invent new words or better ones, because sometimes you come across something and there isn't a word for it. Or perhaps there is, but I haven't read it yet. I mean, why isn't there a word for those days in September when the dew twinkles on the spiders' webs in the privet hedge and the air feels like it's decided just that morning that summer is over? Or the sensation you get when the melted cheese in cheese on toast sticks to the roof of your mouth? I asked Granny that once and she just said, 'Goodness me, Laura, you do have some odd ideas, don't you? Sticky?' and then she gave me a big hug and said 'Bless' to Mum over my head. Sticky's not right: that doesn't describe the way you can push the cheese around with your tongue like playdough and how the butter makes it all slippery.

Mrs Finch has been having 'one-to-ones' with each of us at the moment. One-to-ones are conversations just between her and one pupil, in private. It's part of the preparation for us moving up to secondary school next year. I like Mrs Finch a lot; she reminds me of my Auntie Ruth. She's quite large, like Auntie, and very jolly, with a big laugh that makes her face and boobies bounce up and down. But she can be very strict if she thinks we aren't behaving properly. Everyone knows to keep quiet when Mrs Finch gets one of her moods on. But in the one-to-ones, she is really kind and *empathetic*. That means standing in our shoes and imagining the way we might be feeling. She said, 'Are you nervous about going to Haydon Hill? I know I would be if I were you.' But I'm not, not at all. I'm looking forward to doing new subjects and wearing the Haydon Hill uniform. And anyway, most of my friends are going too, so I don't expect it will be that different there. Mrs Finch said a funny thing when we finished our chat, 'At least you'll never be at a loss for words, Laura,' and gave a little laugh, so I laughed too to be polite and went to collect my coat and bag because it was home time by then.

I was going to call in at the library on my way home, because I knew I would finish *Sense and Sensibility* at the weekend and I was worried I wouldn't have anything to read on Sunday. I want to read all Jane Austen's books and I haven't read *Persuasion* yet, but Granny didn't have a copy of that. 'Still enjoying Miss Austen, then, my pet, are you?' she said last weekend when I rushed back to *Sense and Sensibility* after Sunday lunch and when I said yes, she smiled and whispered, 'I think that's her best book. Takes you to another place, doesn't she?' I knew what she meant. She's taken me to loads of places already – Norland Park, London, Bath, Pemberley, Mansfield Park – so I was looking forward to my next adventure.

But when I came out of school, Mum was waiting at the gate, looking like someone had wiped all the colour off her face. She was peering all around as if she'd lost something, then she saw me and she gave a little cry and broke through the sea of bodies and grabbed me by the wrist. Her hands were icy cold, even though the day was warm. Her mouth was all wobbly and her voice sounded odd, like her tongue was swollen. 'Mum?' I said and my heart jumped in my chest, knocking all the breath out of me.

'It's Granny,' said Mum. 'She's in hospital.' And then we were in the car and Mum was driving in lurches through the traffic and when I looked at her, tears were dripping off her chin on to the front of her shirt. She tried to give me a smile as we pulled into the hospital car park, but it came out all wrong and then she was fumbling in her purse for change to buy a ticket. We ran up the side of the building hand in hand and into the entrance, which was glass and full of light like a cathedral. People were standing and sitting around as if they were waiting for someone to tell them what to do and then Mum was pushing me into a lift and stabbing the button for the fifth floor.

Granny looked very small in the bed. There was something funny about her face. Half of it looked like Granny and half like someone else's face had been stuck on to it, and not very carefully at that. Mum took Granny's hand, which was lying all knotted up on the sheet and stroked it. 'Go on,' she said, nodding her head towards Granny's other hand, 'hold her hand so she'll know you're here.' It felt like tissue paper, all feathery and fragile, like it might tear if you rubbed too hard. 'Dad's on his way,' said Mum. 'And Auntie Ruth.'

I looked at Granny, at the tiny flicker of her eyelids, at the tears leaking out of the eye on the funny side, and I thought of all the things I wanted to tell her about. I wanted to tell her how happy I'd felt when Elinor realises Edward Ferrars really loves her. I thought about the way she always says, 'Goodness me, the speed that child reads!' as if she is a bit embarrassed and a bit proud at the same time. I thought about the day she stopped looking things up in the dictionary for me and pulled the spotty book down from the top of the bookcase and said, 'There you go. That should keep you out of mischief for a while.' I remembered the musty smell when I opened it for the first time and how tiny the words had been and how it was the first time I'd seen the word 'ecstasy' written down and how I told Granny it was my favourite word and she'd smiled.

A nurse came in and murmured something in Mum's ear. Mum got up and whispered to me as if afraid she might wake Granny, 'Dad's on the phone. I won't be long. Talk to Granny while I'm gone.' I must have looked startled, because she leant towards me and said, 'I know she looks like she's asleep, but hearing's the last thing to go.' To go? To go where? And where had the first things gone? What were they? Mum hesitated in the doorway then rushed back to give me a really hard hug. 'Don't be frightened, sweetheart. It's just that at the moment Granny's in another place.'

The sun streamed in through the window, bathing Granny in a white light that almost hurt you to look at it. I sat forward on the hard plastic chair and opened my mouth to say something. I could feel my head buzzing with words, alive with them, but none of them would come out. I thought to myself, I must have thousands, millions of words in my brain, why can't I find any of them? I thought about what Mrs Finch had said and how it wasn't true. I had lost my words. And then I remembered my bag at my feet. I reached down and my hand closed around the book. I knew all about being in another place. I opened Granny's favourite book at my bookmark and, in my best reading-aloud-in-class voice, but quietly so only she could hear, I began to read.

❧

My inspiration: Our son is about to become a father. We were discussing the perfect 'starter library' for our grandchild and reminiscing about how and when we were introduced to certain books. I recalled first reading Jane Austen (and realising on rereading her years later how much I had missed!) and insisted she be included in our collection.

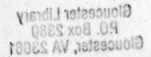

SNOWMELT

Lane Ashfeldt

SNOWMELT

Lane Ashfeldt

'I had thought such ecstasy dead in me forever,
but the sun of Italy has thawed the frozen stream.'
Mary Shelley, 'Rambles in Germany and Italy', 1844

That winter, as snows fell on England and fires raged in Australia, as floods visited both countries, Miss Campbell became convinced the end was near.

She did not say so to neighbours or to people at the library, but the idea was not new to her. For months she had lived in fear of a plague. Scientists were on the alert for a new contagious disease. It was overdue. The next plague to hit would be rapid and deadly, they said. In deference to their opinions she filled two kitchen cupboards with tinned beans and bottled water, enough to survive a month without leaving her loft. She imagined her neighbours in the event of a quarantine. No 'Blitz spirit' for them: they'd be out looting the Tesco Express, the Boots, the Morrisons, even the all-night shop at the garage. When all obvious sources of food and medicine were exhausted, they would attack each other. Her only chance of survival would be to sit tight with her doors and windows locked.

But what form would this new plague take, Miss Campbell asked herself. The avian flu? Some sort of viral cancer? Perhaps, like the Black Death, it had sneaked in at the back door and was quietly multiplying as it fixed itself on the old, the weak and the young. Mr Shanahan, a regular at the library, had been hospitalised at Halloween for laser surgery on his eye. By Christmas he was gone. If she ever needed an operation she would choose day surgery; she did not wish to join the list of superbug victims.

Now, watching the burning bushes and frozen lakes, listening to the signs and portents that issued from her television screen, Miss Campbell began to think that the end of the world might after all be precipitated by something other than a plague. By extreme weather, perhaps: melted ice caps, fire and brimstone, a black sun.

She spent the morning boxing atlases and encyclopaedias. The building she'd worked in for fifteen years had closed its doors, and they had three days in which to stock the new library. Someone came into the reference room and called out, 'Miss Campbell, you here?' She popped her head out from behind the shelf and bumped into Angela from reception.

'Oh. I've a caller asking for the head librarian, but Matt's at a conference. He wants to know when he can set up those PCs in HeadSpace—'

'HeadSpace?'

'You know, the new zone for teenagers. He just needs to confirm an installation slot.'

Oh yes, the room Matt wouldn't let her order any books for. Some grand scheme of his to 'raise the footfall' of young people.

'Very well, I'll speak to him.'

She took the phone and confirmed a time on Thursday.

'Great. So they'll be up and running ahead of the launch,' Angela said.

'Indeed.'

Miss Campbell found it hard to be enthusiastic. She'd hoped to stay on at the library another eight years, until retirement, but her role was changing so fast. Once, her job had been to share her love of books. Not any more. Books, actual physical books made of paper, were becoming a rarity, something to be tucked away in forgotten corners.

That lunchtime she came across a skip in the car park filled with old library hardbacks. Matt had enquired about stock disposal the other day. 'Generally we donate,' she said, but he told her, 'There's additional costs attached and we're over budget on the move.' She spent her lunch break standing on a chair, reaching into the skip to fish out books worth saving. Then she ferried them down the road to Oxfam. It seemed churlish given how much the council was spending, but Miss Campbell couldn't help it: she was going to miss the old library.

The day of the move coincided with a day's annual leave booked months ago. For weeks Miss Campbell had looked forward to this trip. She was taking an evening class on the early novel, and a visit to a library of early women's writing was part of her studies.

Fresh snow had fallen and it glittered on the ground like a Christmas card. The train travelled back in time as swiftly as it raced through frozen fields and copses, until it reached a station whose platforms held no cafés, only painted wooden shelters and matching footbridges. The last stop: the end of the line.

Miss Campbell consulted her map and picked her way down the high street and through the small town, avoiding icy patches and lumps of trodden snow. When she reached the grounds of the house, the whole area was warm and dry. A meadow stretched snow-free and golden into the distance, and a man loaded bales of hay into the loft of a barn as if she'd happened on a small unseasonable patch of summer.

She rang the bell, signed in, climbed the uneven wooden steps and knocked on the library door. A simple room. Books, wooden desks, lamps. A concentrated silence that she longed to bottle and unleash in her own library.

She requested *The Last Man*.

It was an early edition bound in three volumes. Leather edged, with marbled covers and a matching box. She slid the books out, noting that in 1826 the name Mary Shelley still did not appear. By then Percy had been dead a few years and her married name might have helped sales, but the credit was to 'The Author of Frankenstein'. She placed the top book on the foam reader. It opened on the first page.

'Hear you not the rushing sound of the coming tempest?
Do you not behold the clouds open, and destruction
lurid and dire pour down on the blasted earth? See you
not the thunderbolt fall, and are deafened by the shout
of heaven that follows its descent? Feel you not the earth
quake and open with agonising groans, while the air is
pregnant with shrieks and wailings – all announcing the
last days of man?' *

Miss Campbell rose from her seat in alarm. What if this passage from the third volume had revealed itself to her as a warning? A

---

*   *The Last Man*, by The Author of Frankenstein (Mary Wollstonecraft Shelley), Henry Colburn: London, 1826. A copy of this edition is held in the collection at Chawton House Library.

sign. Yes, that was it. The signs were here, but no one could read them. No one wanted to read them.

She hurried to the window, searching for what? A thunderbolt, a quake, a tempest? She half expected to watch the lawn rip asunder, but still it stretched away from the house, green and sunny.

She stood at the window as others had stood before her, going back four centuries. Even before the house existed, local thanes had lived in this area; and before them, Romans, drawn by a warmth they missed from the south.

She breathed deeply.

These ancient words, which might have filled her with terror had she read them alone in her flat at night, were not ready to come true just yet.

Miss Campbell returned to her seat, and to her work. The day passed swiftly, the sun racing across the south lawn to disappear behind the trees. She looked back as she closed the gate; the last light bathed the house and filled the air around it.

On the walk to the station the magic of bygone centuries receded. People on the high street did the same kind of thing people in Balham did — bought naan bread or focaccia, fruit or meat, wine or beer, as they wended their way home. On the train back to the city the sky closed over, a lid slammed on the world.

Descending the steps into the Underground, Miss Campbell was hit by its rich dirty stink. Metallic yet animal. A smell she'd not noticed this morning, it was so long since she'd breathed clean air.

That night she settled in front of her 1973 typewriter and began to type. Earlier she had put off this task, because how can you reduce a person to a few pages, a life and its work to five thousand words? Somehow she felt less wary of her subject now. Spurred on by the noisy rattle of the Golfball, she wrote of Mary Shelley's dark loneliness; her struggles as a single parent; her visions of the end of the world, penned a hundred and fifty years before this typewriter was manufactured, and set another century beyond that in 2073.

'Like *Frankenstein* and horror,' Miss Campbell wrote, '*The Last Man* was conceived before science fiction was a genre, before others trod accepted paths into these strange new worlds. Before leaps in time became pedestrian. Mary Shelley's vision of the future was very different from the one we have today. It had no place for gadgets such as the sonic screwdriver or the improbability drive...'

She typed far into the night, aware and yet unaware of time passing, pausing, rewinding, forwarding.

The following day the computers arrived, and by eleven Miss Campbell was in HeadSpace with the man who had come to install them. Matt, too, was there to see his vision take shape.

'Fantastic, isn't it?'

'I suppose.'

'You don't sound so sure.'

'It's just, we could fit thousands of books in this space, do you know?'

'And I'm sure you know,' he smiled, 'that each computer allows its user to view an infinite number of virtual books?'

'No actual books, though.'

The man installing the machines looked up and the two men exchanged sympathetic glances. Matt declaimed as if a small crowd was gathered round to hear him: 'Isn't what an actual book *is* quite an arbitrary construct? Engravings, wooden tablets, scrolls, vellum sheets, paper: technology moves on, and we must move with it. Change doesn't have to be a bad thing.'

'I like computers,' Miss Campbell said, 'but I like books, too. And I don't think computers can replace them.'

She looked up, curious to see how he'd respond, but by then Matt was sending text messages.

At the launch event she avoided him. Easily done. Matt was busy impressing the local government luminaries who had bankrolled his new library, telling them about the events planned to promote it. They clustered around him, looking even more ironed and dry-cleaned than the librarians, who were at pains to look their best. A champagne reception at work was a rare treat and they were out to make the most of it.

Angela followed Miss Campbell's gaze.

'He's such a high flyer, Matt. I wonder, will he still be with us in six months, or will he move on to some other milestone project?'

'Who cares?' said one librarian.

'Fine by me if he goes,' said another. 'We'll cope without.'

'He gave me a lecture last week on the benefits of change,' Miss Campbell said. 'I took him at his word. I'm selling my flat and moving out of London.'

'Isn't now a bad time to sell?'

'Only the worst for thirty years, they say. But I'm not waiting thirty years for the next good time.'

There was a rush of questions about where she was moving to, and she told them.

'Oh, not such a long commute,' Angela said. 'So you'll stay on here? At the library I mean.' The look she gave Miss Campbell said: don't do anything foolish, my girl.

'Like Matt says – change can be a good thing. There's a little library out that way needs a volunteer. I'll love the work, and if all goes well they'll think of me when a paid vacancy comes up.'

Half disbelieving, half envious, they raised a toast to her new life and the conversation moved on. Later Angela took her to one side.

'If you don't mind my saying, I hope you've thought things through. Doesn't pay to be too impulsive, does it?'

Miss Campbell thought of Mary Shelley. Always hard up. No wonder, since her menfolk were so careless with their finances – but she never let money take over. If she had done there'd be less of interest for a modern reader to learn about her now. As things stood, the time was ripe for a serious in-depth study, and she might just be the person to undertake it.

'Doesn't the danger lie in entrusting our future to others? Like bankers, I mean. Perhaps, Angela, we should take charge—'

'Don't bring "the recession" into this. I'm thinking of you, is all. You don't want to make things hard on yourself.'

Miss Campbell smiled.

'I'm thinking of me, too. I'm thinking, "I only have one life and it could end any time." There are a few things I'd like to do before that happens, do you know?'

Light and shadow flickered across Miss Campbell's face as the train passed a stand of bare-branched trees. Then, in the open fields, the sun steadied and she closed her eyes to focus on its warmth. Already the journey felt familiar. This time she was going south to look for a flat. She had boxed her things in readiness; early that morning a man from Oxfam had come to collect her donation.

'Not the kind of stuff we normally get. Gone off beans, then, have you?' he asked as he lifted the crates of tinned food.

Miss Campbell smiled. She'd stopped believing there was much point in preparing for a plague or for the end of the world. If it came, it came.

He nodded towards the cardboard boxes. 'Those old hardbacks, you'll be wanting them gone too, my love?'

'Oh no,' she said. 'I'll be needing those.'

The train continued south at a leisurely pace. In the sunlight the snow softened and began to dissipate. Brooks and streams, unfrozen, grew brown with snowmelt and brimmed over to lap at fields, their eager ripples forming new and temporary lakes.

My inspiration: The inspiration for this story came from a visit to Chawton House Library one snowy day in February, 2009, to read works by Mary Shelley. *Snowmelt* was also shaped by other recent events in my life and in the world of books, and by a conversation with Chawton House librarian, Jacqui Grainger.

THE WATERSHED

Stephanie Shields

THE WATERSHED

❧

Stephanie Shields

I adopted the brace position from North Cheam to Seaford. Sandwiched between my two older cousins, I only straightened my back to draw air into my constricted lungs. Surreptitiously, Aunt Martha placed two nitroglycerine tablets under her tongue. Maggie, to my left, studied the fleeting verge. James, head tilted slightly to the right, pale-blue eyes abstracted, appeared to be focusing inwards.

Had I been the man who conducts driving tests, I would have sent Uncle Simeon straight back to the centre and prescribed another twenty lessons. Perhaps this was a harsh and arrogant judgement from a seventeen-year-old who didn't drive yet. However, I had driven with my father since I was seven and he exemplified courtesy, common sense and restraint. Uncle Simeon lacked these qualities. If I had to single out the fault beyond all others it was this: he chose, invariably, to overtake in the face of oncoming traffic. This single fault carried a plethora of associated sins. The most embarrassing of these was his compulsion to accompany these near misses with gestures most vulgar, some of which I was unfamiliar with. All school children know the 'V' sign. This he reserved for the milder misdemeanours that he attributed to other, less reckless, road users.

At seventeen, you are particularly susceptible to feelings of acute embarrassment. Cheeks, eyebrows, and a certain set of the lips – each can be a 'giveaway'. Not one to blush, my eyes and mouth were mirrors to my soul. Aunt Martha's lips remained blue throughout the journey – I feared they were the mirror to her heart. She had a soft, kind face, but a spectral pallor and lines of worry and hurt were etched around her eyes and mouth.

Uncle Simeon was exceedingly kind to me. However, kindness should perhaps be viewed with caution if it can be seen as a way of being unkind to others. Towards his own children he was combative and antagonistic; he was a harsh taskmaster and judge.

At this time, I was not entirely at ease with myself. There were a number of reasons for this. Age was certainly one, and the second was this unfamiliar family.

In the early August of this summer of 1966, I was travelling home to Leicestershire from a pleasant, albeit troubled, holiday in Brixham, Devon. My mother was an emotional map reader. She had directed my father further east than we might have anticipated. She loved to break her journey in the Cotswolds; she was particularly fond of tea and scones at the Swan Hotel, in Bibury, so I can only surmise that elements of design and wilfulness had come to the fore in her interpretation of the best route home. Mother had these qualities in abundance. As we passed Basingstoke, she declared we would call on her cousin Simeon Cameron.

My father groaned: 'Why, oh, why?' Exhaustion mingled with exasperation.

'You haven't spoken to him in twenty-three years.'

'Precisely the reason. "Ne'er let the sun go down on thy wrath,"' she quipped, emphatically.

'Excuse me, but the sun's gone down quite a few times since you lot fell out.'

'Look, we're almost at North Cheam, so now is the time. It could be a long time before we pass this way again.'

There were tears of joy and hugs and kisses – ah, sweet reconciliation. The four children, veritable strangers, withdrew from the adults and twenty-three years' worth of catching up and reminiscence, preferring to perambulate the main street of North Cheam. It proved an area conducive for cousinly bonding. We craned to see the interior of the Blue Dragon Chinese Restaurant with its maroon flock wallpaper and gilt sidelights, with red-draped nylon shades and tassels – so exotic. We studied the menu, etched with blue dragons and taped to the window; we chose what we imagined would be our favourite dishes. Chow mein sounded just right for me, with crispy noodles and soy sauce. Opportunities for culinary experimentation were limited in the Leicester suburbs. James and Maggie spoke with greater authority, having sampled some of the dishes off that very menu. My brother David always spoke with authority and plumped for Peking duck.

On our return to the Cameron semi, down the cul-de-sac, I was able to describe the oriental dishes in some detail to my father. He looked appalled. However, Uncle Simeon caught the mood of the moment and proposed a 'takeaway'. Oh bliss! Mother had already forbidden David and me to ever buy anything from the Barbecued Chicken Van that passed our house in Leicester. In retrospect, this was wise. Mother's rationale was based on the limited opportunity for personal hygiene in the van, and the greasiness of the rotating golden chickens. Subsequent history sided with Mum. The barbecued-chicken man was found guilty of lewd behaviour – revealing himself to two young girls from my school. I digress. On this night in North Cheam, Mother cast caution to the wind and was actually seen sucking a spicy spare rib. My own palate had been fine tuned on Vesta paella. Chicken chow mein transported me to a foreign land. My own dragons were held at bay at least for one evening.

Anecdotes, wit, conviviality and a takeaway, and just as we prepared to leave for Leicestershire, Uncle Simeon made a proposal concerning me – that I should stay for a week in North Cheam and that they would return me to Leicester with my cousins, for David's twenty-first birthday party on 15 August.

'That's so kind, and so generous, but I can't possibly. I'm waiting for my results. I must be home.'

Herein lay the third and major reason for my alienation from the world – my impending A level results. The unfairness, the iniquity, the sheer bad luck of the 'trick question' had haunted me throughout the summer. The results were due out on 12 August. My father, always positive, loyal and encouraging, kept saying something about the Glorious Twelfth, but I felt the reverse would be true. My apprehension concerned 'the Watershed'.

I had been studying for English, History and Art A level. I was expected to do best in History and I had worked very hard for all of them, but History had taken a significant amount of revision. Each night I would open the curtains just at the angle to ensure the rising sun would hit my face and wake me early to resume revision. At night, as they went to bed, my parents would come and beg me to stop. But I was driven.

The library curtains wafted in the warm, gentle breeze. They were closed to keep the candidates cool. Linen with a modern pattern – mid-brown with abstract gold, turquoise and pink shapes – variations on a distorted square motif. I studied the paper: 'A watershed in English history—'. Panic paralysed my mind and my pen. What was a 'watershed'? I schooled myself to breathe. How could I answer the question, air my knowledge, if I didn't have a clue what a 'watershed' was? My eyes rotated with fear. I cast about, surreptitiously surveyed my calm companions. I was undone.

The post-examination post-mortem did little to allay my fears, or improve my vocabulary.

'Well, I would have thought it was obvious,' said Mr Robertson, my tutor, quite dismissively.

At home there was discussion. My mother felt that it was a place on a river for keeping boats safe.

'That's a boathouse, my dear.' My father thought it was tough to use such a term. He believed it was connected to rivers dividing, but could not be certain, for wasn't that a confluence?

My brother said that it would be acceptable if I had treated it as a turning point. My red Chambers said, unhelpfully, that it was the line separating two river basins, and, more helpfully, a crucial point or dividing line between two phases. Something in my mind prevented me from revisiting the content of my response. Only disappointment and bafflement remained. I tasted the sour anticipation of failure.

That night there was no opening of the curtains just enough to enable an early start to revision. I felt deflated and dismal. It must have been an hour later I heard my brother's tread on the stairs. There was a soft tap on my door. His head was silhouetted by the landing light. In his mock formal tones he said: 'A boathouse in English history – discuss.'

*

Back to North Cheam, and my newly acquired relatives would brook no opposition to their invitation. I turned to my mother, who saw me as the cement for the resuscitated relationship with her favourite cousin Simeon. I turned to my father. His kind grey eyes batted back my objections – it might take my mind off the results, it would be fun to see the galleries, theatres, Carnaby Street.... He went to fetch my case from the car and slipped me two ten pound notes. He promised he would open my envelope and ring me immediately. The spectre of the envelope on our doormat prompted further dread. Panic coursed round my heart. And I had been abandoned in North Cheam.

James generously moved out of his bedroom; I was installed. A knock at my bedroom door the following morning preceded Uncle Simeon in his mid-calf dressing gown, bearing a cup of tea. I propped myself up in bed and wondered about what they might eat for breakfast. Drawn downstairs by a delicious smell of bacon, I was greeted warmly by the family. Uncle Simeon asked if I'd ever been to Seaford, and I said not. He declared that we would visit it that very day: 'Much more pleasant than Brighton – quieter, more refined and so select.'

Few families can have arrived in Seaford at such speed. It was a relief to disembark. I regained the power in my knees as we walked up towards Seaford Head. The sea shimmered silver, backlit by the morning sun rising in a cloudless sky: silver sea with ice-blue blotches, becalmed, with a fast-evaporating low mist. We walked towards the cut-away cliffs. Thin dark flint strips lined the shocking white chalk face. Gulls whirled high above, calling, and we strained to see them in the bright light. I was entranced. Consciously I drove my demons away and allowed myself to be overwhelmed by the sheer majesty of the moment.

'Why, Uncle, it's beautiful. Look at the light on the sea. Is there a word for the twinkling? A "silver coruscation"?'

Uncle Simeon shrugged, baffled, but he beamed at my delight.

Back in the centre of Seaford cousins called for fish and chips, to be eaten 'alfresco', a new word for me and one I could certainly use with my friends in Leicester. Seaford itself did not disappoint, with its gorgeous vistas and special shops. The family went its various ways and I found a second-hand bookshop on Place Lane, a veritable treasure trove. And there I found it – cerise cover, bonnet in beige with ribbons like tendrils, creeping across the front; black print proclaiming: *Pride and Prejudice* by Jane Austen. One and thruppence was pencilled in the inside cover. This was the treat that I had promised myself for after the exams. I'd held back from securing a copy, fearing defeat. But now I reasoned that it would be better to embark on the novel before my anticipated disappointment could spoil it.

My brown paper bag attracted James's attention.

'What's this then?' He took the package from me and gasped in horror. 'What are you going to do with this?'

'I've always wanted to read it.'

'Even if you don't have to? How weird.'

Maggie sprang to the novel's defence, but James warmed to his theme.

'I had to write an essay for my O level on "The humour of Jane Austen". Imagine that! It's like being asked to write something on snow in summer.'

That evening, back in the bedroom at North Cheam I took my book out of the brown paper bag. I snuffled in the delicious mustiness of its yellowing pages. I began to read. At 1 a.m. I found myself opening the curtains, at just the right angle, for an early start – the first time since the exams.

Each day in North Cheam was like a chocolate plucked from a rich and delicious selection box. Footsore, yet indefatigable, Maggie and I set off, negotiated the Tube, and explored more delights of the capital city. I was entranced and the days passed most pleasantly.

One morning, as I was savouring Elizabeth's interrogation by Lady Catherine de Bourgh at Rosings, I was faintly aware of the telephone ringing downstairs. I was called. It was my father. My knees began to fail me.

'Well, my darling, it certainly is the Glorious Twelfth for you! I am so proud of you, so very well done.'

I sat on the bottom step of the stairs and cried; a quantum shift in my own world had just occurred. No tired return to school in September, for the intended third year in the sixth. A curtain had been drawn open, and there was light.

Later that day I stood before Spencer's 'Resurrection', and felt great awe. I decided to treat Maggie to lunch to celebrate. She steered me to a Lyons Corner House. For 'afters' we had vanilla ice cream, topped with stem ginger, ginger syrup and double cream. It was gorgeous. As I queued to pay the bill, Maggie declared: 'You have done awfully well, you know.' I looked down a little bashfully, and saw my smile reflected in the toes of my new, shiny, black, 'strappy', patent leather shoes.

As we hurtled towards Leicester I sat up proudly in the back of Uncle Simeon's car. We overtook every car on the M1. I reflected on the exhilaration of driving fast and taking risks.

There were already guests arriving at our house. Students had cadged cars, hitched lifts, taken taxis, borrowed vans, and were taking over my home: hairy young men and long-legged girls, squeals of laughter and joy unbounded. I slipped up quietly to my bedroom. One task I had yet to complete. Before the holiday, I had sewn a new silk, Empireline mini dress, in a tiny rose pattern, especially for my brother's party. Mum had marked the hem up for me. I laid it out on the ironing board and systematically turned it up a further inch and three quarters. I hemmed it carefully, and tried it on. There was a soft tap on the door. It was my brother. He hugged me, and then his look took in the whole me. He focused, a little surprised, on the area above my knees. In his mock-formal voice, he quoted:

'Loss of virtue in a female is irretrievable....'

I smiled sweetly, and delivered one of Uncle Simeon's favourite gestures.

My inspiration: Pride and Prejudice and *Mansfield Park* inspired this tale of an artless seventeen-year-old girl's 'watershed' week. Her known world is the confined society of the Leicester suburbs. She awaits her A level results, convinced of failure. Her world view is changed by an unexpected, unsought and initially unwanted week in London, staying with unfamiliar relatives. A second-hand copy of *Pride and Prejudice,* secured for 'one and thruppence', sustains her. Her wilful mother and kindly father owe something to the Bennets. However, it is the reckless Uncle Simeon who is the catalyst for her transformation.

SOMEWHERE

Kelly Brendel

SOMEWHERE

❧

Kelly Brendel

I must remember to be back in time for Dr Grant's dinner. The excitement of the young people for putting on a play is hard to resist, the thrill of it all so contagious; but if I am not there while it is prepared cook will surely end up shouting and snapping at the new scullery maid. Poor Lizzy, only fifteen but clumsy and, as cook claims, always underfoot; not a day seems to pass that there isn't an explosion of curses and crying from the kitchen that I must rush to calm and soothe.

Today, however, our cast rather seems to have dispersed and I've found myself wandering the house aimlessly. Mrs Norris has been curiously absent from the afternoon's events, for normally she loves to be in the thick of a bustle caused largely by herself, or else haranguing poor Miss Price. While the morning passed in an animated flurry of scene changes, forgotten lines and eager chatter the afternoon has been quiet... so quiet that I begin to feel something creep up on me.

Mr Bertram and his 'intimate friend' Mr Yates have been bickering in the newly converted billiards room this past hour about the play. For Bertram everybody spoke too slow, for Yates

135

too quick, they were playing it with too much pathos, nay not enough for Yates and it was only when Mr Rushworth stepped up to ask how he might help that they were silent. Julia has passed by now and again to glower upon the general theatrical proceedings, although always leaving promptly when she catches Yates's eager eye. Hopefully she has gone to seek out Henry, for I have not seen him since lunch.

I can't help but smile at my matchmaking plans for Mary and Henry. That first evening Dr Grant and I were invited to dine with all those at the great house (a note urging our presence had been issued by Mrs Norris on behalf of her sister Lady Bertram that brooked no refusal) I had looked around the assembled faces and with an eye that strayed to the eldest Bertram son thought of Mary. Marriage to Dr Grant had not blinded me to Mr Bertram's good looks, rather the contrast of them sitting to supper across the same table threw his looks into sharper focus. Heir to a great estate and in possession of a kind of laughing good humour, he would well suit Mary's vivacity and wit. I accepted Mary's later proposal of a visit with alacrity and who can blame me if my thoughts strayed to matrimony for her? Henry, too, I thought could find his happiness at Mansfield, for Miss Julia Bertram was a fine, good-humoured girl who would suit him, I was sure.

My guesses went slightly awry when Mary began to care for the younger Bertram son, Edmund; his admiration touching and inciting hers. Yet I am not so proud as to resent the collapse of my prediction. She glows with the flush of romance and I look upon it with a joy of my own. As for Henry, he, I'm sure, likes Miss Julia, though when I mention this to Mary she only smirks and looks archly towards the eldest Miss Bertram.

Yes, these love intrigues do make me wonder. What shall become of them all? My own time of intrigue does not offer such a charming show. We met at one of his sermons; my seat in the fourth row, squeezed between my mother and old Mrs Dandridge, whose foggy breath rasped wheezily in the cold November church, was not a conducive setting for romance, nor was his sermon itself made of the stuff to set hearts beating or my own thoughts stirring. But his gentle attentions caused a flutter of pride and satisfaction, my mother was gently approving and my plain self had never experienced or expected to experience a man's admiration. But I was married to him three months later.

That first night, trembling in my bridal blush, I swear I saw him balk and shudder, daintily picking at my clothes like the morsels of last night's dinner in the flickering light. Dr Grant took to his marital duties with little zeal and that night I shuddered too and started away from him before growing still.

Yet I was fairly happy. There were pleasures in having a house of my own. All I had to do to keep Dr Grant contented was ply him with a selection of choice dishes, the best of which he would commend with a hearty burp. There was much to occupy me in furnishing the house, visiting the surrounding families, making friends for myself in the village and cultivating my garden. There I can lose myself amongst the flowers that burst and reveal themselves in a flourish of colour - searing their sights upon my dazzled eyes. Mary and Henry's coming was a welcome distraction however, just as I was beginning to feel something stirring unbidden in me - yes, their arrival was very welcome.

In all my wandering I seem to have reached the upper landing and I hear the soft murmurs of a scene taking place. I creep towards the door, partly cracked open, through which light and voices are spilling. Mary and Edmund are standing rather close together, only two feet between them, facing each other. They are rehearsing a scene from *Lovers Vows*, their eyes and burning cheeks bent to the pieces of paper in their hands. I know the scene. It is their scene. Edmund spoke his line then:

'When two sympathetic hearts meet in the marriage state, matrimony may be called a happy life. When such a wedded pair finds thorns in their path, each will be eager, for the sake of the other, to tear them from the root. Patience and love will accompany them in their journey, while melancholy and discord they leave far behind— Hand in hand they pass on from morning till evening, through their summer's day, till the night of age draws on, and the sleep of death overtakes the one. The other, weeping and mourning, yet looks forward to the bright region where he shall meet his still-surviving partner, among trees and flowers which themselves have planted, in fields of eternal verdure.'

There followed a moment of silence in which Mary did not seem able to speak. I could not wonder at this. The fervent, almost reverent tone in which Edmund spoke before his passion spent itself and sank his voice into a tremulous whisper had moved even me, the offstage observer peeping through a crack in the door. Mary managed to answer but her voice was strange to me when she spoke.

'You may tell my father... I'll marry.'

Their eyes, as if by some communion moved up from the paper and to each other.

'This picture is pleasing; but I must beg you not to forget that there is another on the same subject. When convenience and fair appearance, joined to folly and ill humour, forge the fetters of matrimony, they gall with their weight the married pair. Discontented with each other – at variance in opinions – their mutual aversion increases with the years they live together. They contend most where they should most unite; torment, where they should most soothe. In this rugged way, choked with the weeds of suspicion, jealousy, anger, and hatred, they take their daily journey, till one of these *also* sleep in death. The other then lifts up his dejected head, and calls out in acclamations of joy – oh, liberty! Dear liberty!'

I started and moved away from them. I had stayed too long after all, it was rude to watch, and suppose Mary or Edmund happened to look up and see me spying through the door, how would that look? But why should I feel my cheeks burn, throbbing with some strange and violent heat, and why that tight clenching in my stomach? Why — it's as if I had just been caught in the act of something shameful. Nothing had been said, they were only the worthless lines from a play; they were invented, unreal, and had no reason to make me press against the wall and gasp for breath. Dr Grant and I were not unhappy after all, he was not a bad husband or unkind. Really we rubbed along quite well together. He has his bursts of temper to be sure and at such moments I can sense, rather than see, Mary and Henry's exchanged looks. Yet they do not take into account the whole picture. He has sense and is considerate for my comfort; when not disturbed by some culinary mishap he can be very pleasant company. There were times in the beginning when my gnawing miseries consumed me utterly... but they were all in the past. Now I have things to occupy me, to make me — no, not happy perhaps but content and, if not always content, if there are occasions when I still yearn for more, when long hours are spent awake burning and bristling in the night, I am always comfortable.

I wasn't quite quick enough in moving away to miss a murmured '"I am in love"' from Mary. Her character or her words?

For I rather think poor Mary is in love, for all her fashionable airs that laughingly disclaim anything like affection she is as caught as Edmund. Hardly a night passes that she doesn't burst into my room before we all settle down for bed; to talk over the day's events, to spear the follies of those at the house upon her wit, but most of all to speak of Edmund. And when she doesn't speak of him she speaks around him, as if all she thinks and says is framed around that sacred spot he occupies. She laughs and chatters and dazzles, pacing about my room in an almost manic frenzy of joy. She is alive and exulted with love. Her talk is all for Edmund and when we visit the house daily now her eyes are all for Edmund too.

Yet I have more to look forward to, real joys that quicken and breed with each passing day. To have a child of my own. I have only recently coerced Dr Grant to try for a baby and though there has been no joy yet, I feel a powerful certainty that tells me it shall be soon. For now there is a little girl in the village named Catherine, or Kitty as I call her. I go to her every few days and sit with her for a couple of hours, and when I hold her I think of the child I haven't yet had. There is a pang in this. There must always be a pang. But there is delight too. Even the storms and rages of her tantrums become a pleasure as, in the moments after, while I soothe her on my knee, she clings to me with such passionate desperation. Could a lover do such, all fickle caresses and empty words? Can a few enchanted hours, hazy with love, eclipse this?

I've moved downstairs and can hear the voices of the others now, they have come. For a moment I imagine them as my avid audience watching my entrance, eager to see my great performance. But when I brush through the doorway they are clustered about in a circle only looking at each other. Still I move towards them gratefully, almost greedily, eager for their bright, light talk and the warmth of their company. A flicker of my eye spies Miss Price by the window, half obscured by the careful draping of the curtain. Mr Rushworth is with her, stuttering and stumbling over his lines. Yet for once Miss Price is not carefully attending to him; tirelessly listening, nodding and correcting his lines without a flicker of impatience as is her wont. Instead her gaze is absently contemplating something in the distance, replaying some scene of the past or of her own imagination. There is something stricken and almost fierce in her gaze that both calls to and answers me. For a moment we lock eyes and share a long, measured look. Yes there it is, there I am - but before I falter I turn away.

Mr Bertram's voice swells over the other's chatter briefly and I catch his words: 'Come now, Yates, we all have our parts to play and you must play yours. No more of your sly evasions and—'

His words fall then and become lost among the general din; yet they continue to reverberate within me. Yes, Mr Bertram, we do all have our parts to play. For Mary, my Mary, there will be nothing but the centre stage, the sun of Edmund's love upon her, she will burst and bask and revel in its glorious rays. I can feel its reflections even offstage. I imagine how it must feel and for a moment, imagining, can almost feel it too.

For me in the wings awaits a wilting darkness, but the mask will never slip. I will take my cue and not miss a line, no matter if no one is attending. Yet I will not shroud myself in misery, I may blaze with my own joys too. In the darkness I will search out my happiness for myself, uproot it before I wither. One must find their comforts and I will find mine. Somewhere. Everywhere. But now I really must be home in time for Dr Grant's dinner.

❦

My inspiration: I was inspired by the following passage in *Mansfield Park*, spoken by Mrs Grant: 'There will be little rubs and disappointments everywhere, and we are all apt to expect too much; but then, if one scheme of happiness fails, human nature turns to another; if the first calculation is wrong, we make a second better: we find comfort somewhere.'

THE OXFAM DRESS

Penelope Randall

THE OXFAM DRESS

Penelope Randall

Kelsey, Lucy, Bex. And Charlie.

The problem was cash, or rather, the lack of it. Charlie didn't have the means to Keep Up, so one day soon three beautiful friendships must end. A chunk of her world would vaporise and vanish. When this mood hit her Charlie pictured light sabres from Star Wars. *Ker-pow.* Just like that.

Kelsey, Lucy, Bex and Charlie. Charlie let them down, and not just with money. For one thing she enjoyed doing homework, and for another there was her hair. It was a) red and b) unstraightenable. Persistent offences for which she must eventually pay the price.

She guessed this ought to bother her more than it did.

'Charity shops are cool,' she suggested one lunchtime, while they were sitting in Subway digesting the warm smells of mass-produced bread and too many fillings. They watched Bex growing bored with her salami and brie. She'd begun picking out olives and flicking them into a soggy heap on the table top.

Kelsey, newly-blonded and with a sufficient coating of fake tan to insulate her from most of life's barbs, tapped her lip. 'Why?'

'Good places to buy from,' Charlie said. Of them all, Kelsey had the most disposable cash; at their school wealth seemed to come in inverse proportion to brains. Charlie quietly hugged to herself the fact that none of the others knew what inverse proportion meant. Charlie was in the top maths set, with the nerdy girls who wanted to do it for A level.

'Buying is like giving them a donation. And you end up with something you want. Maybe a bargain.' She nibbled regretfully at an olive. It was always hopeless to mention how little you'd spent on something. Admiration, after all, went simply and directly in line with price.

As if to press home this obvious truth Bex wrinkled her nose. 'Why would you want to?' Bex's teeth were tanked with wire, as if her opinions needed shoring up.

'There's this blue dress in Oxfam.'

Lucy's phone buzzed with an incoming text. Lucy was tall and naturally golden and used to play tennis for the school before she got too cool for sport.

'Josh passed his driving test!'

It was summer, GCSEs, and Year Eleven was drawing to an anxious and disorientating close. Charlie got up at seven-thirty every morning and did an hour's revision before breakfast. The others lay in bed until lunchtime unless they had an exam, when they'd need time in front of the mirror with straighteners and lip gloss, texting each other about how little they knew. Panic was a competitive sport.

'I don't get it,' Kelsey moaned as they left Subway. It took twelve-and-a-half minutes to walk to school. 'LECDs. Tell me.'

'LEDCs,' Bex said. 'Less Economically Developed Countries.'

'Less than what?'

'Than MEDCs. It's on the front of the exam paper.'

'So, they're, like, poor.'

The girls rounded the corner by the post office and the school gates slid into view. Charlie read the latest from Lucy's phone.

'Josh is getting a car.'

Josh was big and dark and beautiful, with hair down to his shoulders and a bum in his rugby shorts that might have been carved from teak. During the winter they'd all taken to watching rugby on Thursday nights, parading their handwoven scarves and slouch boots along the touchline. They'd learned phrases like drop goal and forward pass. There was a bit of a frisson about walking into the boys' school, from all the hormones that got mixed with the floor polish in the corridors. Little boys at the lockers gawped as they went past. Sometimes the teachers did too, but they never said anything, not if you'd come to watch sport. Boys' schools encouraged that kind of thing.

'He wants a Mini Cooper. One of those new ones.'

Josh was also Lucy's unreachable stepbrother. He occupied a separate and unimaginable stratospheric orbit, coddled by other grey suits and yellow-striped sixth form ties, worn wide and loose and sexy. Kelsey, Lucy, Bex and Charlie picked out names to decorate their school planners in highlighter pens and Tipp-Ex. Ben, Josh, Grant, Callum. They sought information from Facebook but none of the boys added them as a friend.

Worse, the rugby season had ended months ago.

Eighty-four girls in damp white shirts huddled in the school foyer, clutching biros and rulers.

'Hey. Megan looks scared.' Kelsey nudged Bex.

'Scared she'll get less than ninety-nine percent.'

Charlie turned to glance at Megan, who sat behind her in maths and barely spoke. Megan had waist-length hair that no one remembered ever being cut. It was as greasy as chip fat and had a halo of split ends.

'No time to shower when there's LEDCs to learn,' Bex murmured, but somehow loud enough for everyone to hear.

Charlie knew, because her mum talked to Megan's mum – they lived on the same estate and had younger siblings who walked to the primary school two streets away – that Megan washed her hair sometimes twice a day, and took medication for her acne. The drugs she'd been prescribed were so dangerous you had to do a pregnancy test before they let you have them. Even if you'd never had a boyfriend.

She hadn't mentioned any of this to Kelsey and Lucy and Bex.

From her corner Megan smiled at Charlie, the sort of woebegone little smile that made Charlie want to team up with Bex and squirt superglue into Megan's ponytail. Although of course there were days when she thought of rallying Megan so that together they could gather all the Ugg boots and designer handbags and chuck them in Lost Property with the old gym shorts and rancid lunchboxes. Occasionally Megan walked to school with Charlie, but usually her dad gave her a lift so she didn't have to walk anywhere with anyone. Charlie held up crossed fingers and grinned non-committally, jiggling her pens.

'Don't encourage her,' Kelsey hissed.

Afterwards, numbed by Geography, they reeled into Starbucks. Bex and Lucy ordered iced cappuccinos. Charlie, who had to rely for cash on her Saturday job at the newsagent's, leaned on the counter and read a message from her phone.

What did u think? Last q was murder r u @ kelsey's?

Megan was the only person Charlie knew who used

apostrophes in her texts. She flipped the Back button to hide the screen and watched Lucy rearranging her hair in a fresh cascade of glossy clichés. Vibrant. Glowing. Because She Was Worth It.

Sometimes Charlie managed to think of her own hair as *pre-Raphaelite*. Days like this it was just frizzy, and badly conditioned to boot.

'There was this top in Monsoon,' Bex began loudly. Charlie sighed.

'Come with me to look at that dress?' she said to Kelsey.

Charlie's mum worked in the Oxfam shop on Wednesday afternoons and gave Charlie a lift home at the end of the day if she didn't mind hanging around for an hour, helping with the stock.

Today was Thursday.

As Kelsey crossed the threshold her face actually puckered, like she needed a pomander to stuff under her nose. It seemed to Charlie, annoyingly, that the clothes in the shop were thinner and more lifeless than usual. Granny garments, and not in the nice, retro, *antique* sense, like twenties lace or a real cloche hat. This stuff was more printed polyester and jersey knits in poisonous patterns. She hooked the blue dress off its rail.

She'd remembered it as silky, but now she saw that the fabric was cheap and stiff, its colour an electric ultramarine rather than the pale indigo she'd held in her head. Which was annoying because Charlie had a knack for recalling shades. She'd arrive at art lessons with colour schemes memorised and ready to put to paper. She got them right, too. Charlie was hoping to do Art for A level. They all wanted to, but in Bex's and Kelsey's and Lucy's cases it was because there was nothing else they liked. And they thought Art was easy.

'Well?' Charlie draped the dress over her arm, knowing that

Art was actually impossible. How could anyone look at something you'd created for an exam and give it a *mark?* A mere number?

Kelsey shrugged. 'It's up to you.'

'I think,' Charlie retaliated archly, 'that I may as well buy it.'

Behind the cash desk were pictures of African people with goats and spice baskets and piles of woven blankets in sunburned colours. The assistant reached forward and Charlie noticed too late that it was Malcolm, the work-experience boy with the speech impediment, whose mouth didn't ever seem to close properly. He always had a fine thread of drool running down the side of his chin. Malcolm used to be Special Needs and now Charlie's mum supervised him at work. Sometimes he helped Charlie with the stock check. It took ages longer.

'Pretty,' Malcolm declared, running the fabric of the dress across his hand. 'It'll suit y— y— you.' The expression on Kelsey's face drilled loudly through the back of Charlie's head.

'Working Thursday this week, Malcolm?' She pulled her shoulders into line. Vital not to show weakness.

'Ei— Ei— Eileen's off. She's at a we— we— wedding.'

Charlie wrenched her purse from her blazer pocket.

'It's in I— I— Ireland.'

'That's nice.' She realised now that the dress was dreadful, beyond any hope of resurrection through minor means such as a change of buttons or a new neck insert of cotton lace. Why had she ever imagined that might work?

'Seven pounds p— p— please,' said Malcolm. He was staring at Kelsey without apprehension. He carried on staring.

It struck Charlie like a giant paper dart soaked in cold water. *He fancies her.* The idea was so awful she thought the whole room might actually implode. They'd all be buried neck-deep in hideous garments and ethically-sourced chocolate bars.

Worse, any moment now poor Malcolm would be telling them about his newest computer game, or even the buses he'd spotted in his lunch hour. Charlie had a ten pound note in her hand, practically her entire remaining earnings from Saturday. She banged it down on the counter. 'I don't want the change.' Then she bolted for the door, ushering Kelsey's attention towards a poster in the window.

'"Ten pounds buys three sacks of seeds for a poor farmer."'

'Oxfam shops. Good places to spend money.'

It was Josh. Impossibly just there, on the pavement, ranged with Ben and Grant and Callum. Looking like they'd dropped off the cover of Cool Guys Monthly.

You could hear Kelsey's brain changing gear. She gained three inches in height and more in chest size. 'It's, like, you're giving them a donation,' she declared. 'For poor people in *LEDCs*.'

Josh nodded. 'What did you buy?'

Charlie rearranged her grip on her bag and relaxed into the spectacle of Kelsey's orange face working overtime while her mouth remained obstinately slack.

Charlie's phone buzzed.

'Megan?' Instead of relief at the change of topic, Kelsey's lower lip displayed asymmetric derision.

Revise quadratic equations tonite?

Then Josh – they were still here, Josh and Ben and Grant and Callum – kicked thoughtfully at a bit of gravel. 'Megan Edwards?'

'Yes.'

'Paul Edwards's sister?'

Kelsey glanced at Charlie.

'Yes.' Charlie realised that Kelsey, Bex and Lucy had no idea of Paul's existence. Megan's older brother was barely seen in real life.

He was thin and gangly and had rosy, hairless skin like a toddler.

'Going to Cambridge,' Josh went on. 'Natural Sciences. Fast bowler.'

Thus was Paul Edwards alternatively defined. Ben's and Grant's and Callum's feet scraped the pavement in agreement.

There was a pause, and Charlie waited for some recollection from Kelsey of best friendship with Megan and Paul. Aligning herself for reflected glory was an accomplishment, sometimes jaw-droppingly effective.

And it was always a mistake to underestimate her.

'Last exam tomorrow,' Kelsey began, her utterance of the word knocking Charlie off-balance. 'Maths. Anyone like to help me out?'

Charlie fingered her phone. 'Actually—'

'Josh,' Kelsey rounded on him, chemically aglow. 'You're a maths bod.'

He smiled back. 'We have nets this evening.'

'What?'

'Cricket practice. Team selection for the weekend.'

'Oh. Yeah.'

Charlie blinked as Kelsey failed to grasp the implications. The boys turned to walk away and jagged lines appeared around them. The sun became unexpectedly brighter. Charlie imagined a migraine would be like that. Or an acid trip.

Cricket. Why hadn't they thought of it?

She flipped open her phone, scrolled to Megan's text and pressed Reply.

Warm, grassy afternoons. Cold beer. No more exams. Leg before wickets and no balls and silly mid-offs. It surely wasn't rocket science to mug up on this stuff. You just had to have some working brain cells. The right connections. A plan.

With enough determination, tables could be turned. Flipped right over – if your friendships were already fatally flawed. Thinking hard, Charlie twisted a strand of uncooperative red hair around her forefinger and yanked it tight.

Ouch.

Kelsey, Lucy and Bex always knew what they wanted, and grabbed it.

Four doors further down the street Charlie skipped into the Age Concern shop and dropped the blue dress into a box by the counter. After a moment she did the same with her school blazer. Recycling, she thought happily. Setting things in motion all over again, somewhere around the loop.

My inspiration: An apparently anachronistic scene from *Pride and Prejudice* in which the Bennet sisters are discussing a shopping trip. Lydia defends her impulsive acquisition of a bonnet: 'I thought I might as well buy it as not...there were two or three much uglier in the shop...' My story puts a modern day spin on such essential teenage issues as vanity, flirting and the ill-considered purchase of unattractive garments.

MARIANNE AND ELLIE

Beth Cordingly

MARIANNE AND ELLIE

※

Beth Cordingly

Ellie sat, book in hand, trousers around her ankles, momentarily winded by the familiar words:

> *A lover's eyes will gaze an eagle blind;*
> *A lover's ears will hear the lowest sound,*

They came like bad news in an unexpected phone call, disarming her. Flicking to the front page of the book she saw her father's shambolic scrawl and felt a pang of envy that it was in her sister Marianne's possession. Simultaneously she heard his voice in her head reciting the lines like a mantra. It was he who had underlined the section and placed the red leather bookmark within those pages: he who had taught his daughters to be open to love and to 'never settle,' quoting from Shakespeare to illustrate his point. And Marianne, despite breaking off her engagement and fleeing to a rented bedsit, had dutifully placed *The Hundred Greatest Love Poems Ever* somewhere it would be seen daily – as reading material in her new bathroom. To stay open to love, Ellie supposed.

She washed her hands thoughtfully; the words ringing like a melody stuck in her head; her father's lilting tones both a comfort and a menace. She couldn't work out how to *be* now, on leaving the bathroom. She had thought to find a laughable cliché about love and emerge triumphant, chastising her sister for keeping such a silly book in her loo. Yet here she was, disrupted by Shakespeare and gulping back tears. It had brought something back, a value: a benchmark. Now was not the time. Ellie was supposed to be the sensible one. Her sister looked to her for answers.

Marianne sat slumped by the kitchen table in the same position she had shuffled to at ten o'clock that morning, a cloudy cup of tea beside her, cold. A blue towelling dressing gown hung limply about her and her bed-head fringe stuck up like a shoot from an onion. The bedsit was small, a waist-high partition dividing the bed from the kitchen and the curtains were still drawn despite it now being past noon. As Ellie re-entered the room, inhaling the stale air of unwashed feet and sleep, Marianne lifted glazed eyes to meet hers. For a moment, with her spindly fingers, grey skin and sorrowful, helpless look she reminded Ellie of ET.

'What am I going to do?' the piteous figure whispered for perhaps the fourteenth time that morning, crashing her forehead down into her palms. Cloistered away here for two days, Ellie was running out of tactics with which to distract her from The Disaster. They had been over and over the positives: Marianne hadn't sent the invites out, she hadn't been humiliated at the altar, it was better than a divorce in three years time, Uncle John hadn't been asked to give her away yet. Lawrence's backtrack decision that he 'wasn't ready' had not come as a huge surprise to anyone except Marianne but that was probably not a helpful observation at this point.

It could not be said that Ellie shared her sister's distress at the prospect of no longer embracing Lawrence into their family. A charming yet flirtatious actor he owned an air of expectancy that

Ellie found exhausting. One was expected to be eternally grateful for the sprinkling of stardust Lawrence might occasionally cast in your direction. Marianne had found this self-importance enigmatic and alluring but to be fair, Ellie reasoned, there was something of their father in his charisma that would appeal to her sister. Lawrence lacked a sense of the world having any meaning other than how it did or did not serve him. But so, in a way, did Marianne. The main problem, Ellie was sure, and the reason the relationship was doomed from the start was encapsulated by something her father had once said. It was the reason he gave for marrying their mother, a schoolteacher with no theatrical ambition.

'Actors shouldn't go out with actors,' he'd decreed, 'It doesn't work.' You can't have two centres of the universe.' Unfortunately Marianne disregarded this part of her father's legacy, being naturally drawn to the drama that only intense personalities can invoke.

Over yesterday's mugs of tea Ellie had tentatively tried to suggest to the blue-gowned form that perhaps what she needed was the opposite to a 'Lawrence'. Someone she wouldn't have to compete with, who was attentive and happy to rest in her shadow. Someone firm but not a threat. And not an actor. Someone, it occurred to Ellie in a moment of clarity that she did not mention out-loud, like a male version of herself.

It proved too early to introduce the concept of moving on. Marianne had listened and nodded sagely but on opening her mouth to speak she had managed only a wail and the same four words to which she had gained a firm attachment, "But I love him".

Rocking her sister gently, Ellie was pondering whether it would be insensitive to ask if she could open a window when Marianne raised her head and asked her a question she could not answer.

'I am twenty-eight years old,' she announced solemnly, 'and I was thinking... if I were to meet myself when I was eighteen, say, in the street or in a café, what would she think of me?'

Ellie blinked but said nothing, unsure whether Marianne was about to enlighten her or if this was a participatory exercise. It was sometimes difficult to tell whether Marianne was genuinely interacting or on the verge of a great soliloquy. She was staring straight ahead, leading Ellie to believe that it was indeed a rhetorical question when suddenly she turned, grasping Ellie's hands and glaring with a crazed urgency into her eyes.

'*What* would she think of me?' she repeated and then, more alarmingly, 'and what would *yours* think of *you*?' It was not so much the question itself that concerned Ellie as the tone of disgust with which it was delivered.

'What do you mean?' Ellie asked, frowning slightly.

'Oh, don't be like that, El,' Marianne's eyes began to twinkle, 'Don't go all wounded soldier. I'm just saying. *You* are fine. You are always fine. Good, sensible Elinor with your sensible, proper job and your lovely, cosy boyfriend. And your Borough Market coffee.'

There was a pause. Marianne had a unique way of making a compliment sound like an insult.

'And?'

'And... look at what you were like when you were eighteen!'

Ellie shrugged, blankly.

'Oh come *on,*' persisted her persecutor, 'you were anti-establishment, anti-men, a commitment-phobe...you were terrified of everything!'

Ellie looked away. It was generally easier to go along with assumptions Marianne made about her life than to contradict her with the truth. Whatever part of her soul her sister was attempting to dissect, the event would pass quicker if she didn't engage.

'And now, silly, you're the happiest, most secure person I know. It's…well, it's wonderful.' Tears welled in Marianne's eyes and she squeezed Ellie's hand, willing her to agree.

'Why do you have to do that?' Ellie was uncharacteristically abrupt.

'What?'

'Make my life sound…somehow lesser because I don't indulge in Histrionics.'

Marianne widened her eyes.

'What do you mean? I was – I was saying—'

'I know what you were saying, Marianne. You were saying that my life is boring and aren't I lucky to have escaped the trauma of *passion* and all the things that you and Dad and actors and artistic people *feel*? Well, just because I'm a scientist it doesn't mean I can't appreciate poetry. And it doesn't mean I don't have feelings and it doesn't mean my relationship is… boring or perfect. We have arguments, we have… I—'

She stopped, her face hot, her throat closing up. She sensed tears coming and felt stupid. Hysteria was her sister's domain. 'Marianne needs a lot of looking after,' their mother had said one Christmas day. They had been waiting for half an hour for Marianne to appear for Christmas dinner but the roars of anguish coming from her bedroom told of new dramas with the boyfriend of the time. Their father had gone up to try to talk her down but had got caught up in it and not reappeared. Everyone indulged Marianne.

'Wellie, don't be cross with me,' Marianne was sobbing, 'I only meant I wish I had what you had. I wish I did—'

Ellie berated herself. In her sister's present state it was appropriate that everyone else appeared to be living a life she no longer had access to. Now was clearly not the time for Ellie to disclose that her own relationship was in trouble.

'Oh *god*,' Marianne let out a wail, 'What if there's someone else? I can't bear it, Ellie. I can't. What am I going to do?'

Silently Ellie re-cradled her sister and gave over her décolletage to soaking up the tears.

At half past three Marianne was on the phone to their mother, repeating every thought and feeling as if the past twenty-four hours of Ellie's counsel had never happened. Ellie wrote her a note.

'Going Waitrose for supplies. HAVE A SHOWER!!! Leaving at six. See you in 20 mins.'

She had lied to Marianne that she was meeting Richard later. Devotion to a lover was the only excuse Marianne would accept unquestioningly in order for her to leave. Richard was territory with whom she could not compete. In reality Richard would work late and when he eventually made it home, Ellie would have to feign sleep. The argument they had had the week before had opened up a chasm small enough to gloss over but too big to revisit and this was what was called 'getting on with life'.

Stepping into the crisp sunshine of Marylebone High Street, Shakespeare's words returned to unbalance her.

A lover's eyes will gaze an eagle blind;

Ellie stood staring into the road. That a lover should be so enthralled by the subject of its affection that it could gaze for eternity into their eyes. It had hit her as some sort of blinding confirmation of her fears. Had she and Richard ever gazed like that? It was there, still there, it had to be. She called him.

'Hi, Ellie.'

'Rich,' she began, 'I just wanted to say that I love you. And I'm sorry and I just want everything to be okay—'

He said nothing.

'I love you. I just…wanted you to know.'

'Ell, I can't talk about this now.'

'I know, I know you can't.' She felt defensive. Silly.

'But I have been thinking about stuff and we'll talk,' he continued, sounding far away and contained. 'The problem is, Ellie, your default reaction is always that it's not good enough. And I can't live like that. I want to be enough.'

'You are enough,' Ellie heard her voice squeak, but even as she spoke the words, she doubted herself.

Back at the bedsit Ellie poured red wine. She had not divulged why she was staying another night and Marianne had not pushed her.

'It's funny,' she remarked, seemingly apropos of her sister's situation, 'you meet and fall in love with all these things about a person and then you tussle for two, three years, trying to turn them into something else… to get them to understand what you need or want. And you sort of use each other up. And then, finally, when you both understand each other, it's like you're spent. And it's too late.'

Marianne eyed her sister solemnly.

'Yes,' she agreed, 'it's like training a dog. And the worst bit is that then someone else – the next person – comes along and benefits from all your hard work.'

There was a pause as they contemplated this unsatisfactory injustice.

'The only good thing I can think is that it's cyclical,' Marianne continued, 'The next girl Lawrence meets will think he's wonderful until she becomes his girlfriend and he begins flirting with everything that moves. Then she'll develop paranoia and turn into me.'

'What if the next girl can cope with the way he is?'

'Then she's right for him and I'm not,' Marianne replied, in a rare moment of self-awareness. 'It's horrific,' she added, 'I'm not doing it anymore.'

Ellie laughed. 'If you're not doing it anymore then why have you put Dad's book of love poetry in the bathroom? You're doing what Dad always told us – to invite love in, to attract it—'

'No. It's the opposite. It's to remind me that love is a construct.'

'You don't think love's a construct.'

'I do. I'm turning into you.'

'I don't think love's a construct!'

'Okay, keep your hair on.'

'No, don't do that. Don't put that on me. You don't know what I think. I do believe in love, I do want to – to – gaze—' she stopped. It sounded weak on her tongue. Marianne pounced.

'I saw you'd been looking at that, Dad's favourite poem—'

'So?'

'I saw you'd been reading it.'

'Well then you'll agree. It's about an ideal, something we aspire to. Gazing an eagle blind. Don't tell me you don't believe in that because you do, we all do. It messes us up because we want it so badly.'

Marianne smiled, triumphant, 'You're wrong, Dad got it wrong. I read the notes at the back. It's not about that. Eagles were meant to be the only birds that could stare directly at the sun without going blind. It means a lover's eyes are brighter than the sun and a lover's ears can hear things that even a thief will miss.'

'Yes—'

'Meaning a lover's senses are more honed – more paranoid – than anyone else's.'

'Meaning?'

'Meaning that as lovers we are doomed to be paranoid freaks. It's not a happy affirmation of love, it's a condemnation.'

Ellie looked at Marianne. Why try to melt the barriers she had put in place for her own protection? They would not hold for long. And knowing Lawrence the chapter would not be closed until sufficient melodrama and his desire for what he had now made unobtainable had played out. What Ellie currently needed to believe in, Marianne needed to deny. And Marianne needed more looking after.

'Either way,' Ellie began carefully, 'it seems to be saying that love is something we should immerse ourselves in…that consumes us. In a good way or a bad way.'

'I was consumed,' Marianne said, her voice splintering into a bleat as her eyes filled up once more.

'I know, darling,' Ellie said quietly and poured more wine.

⁂

My inspiration: In *Sense and Sensibility* there is a moment where Elinor nurses Marianne's broken heart whilst concealing that she suffers one too. I wanted to explore a modern-day version of *Sense and Sensibility* where two sisters of opposing temperaments discuss the nature of love. As with Austen's characters they are eloquent and well read but these present day heroines have professions, are older and live independently. I have aimed to maintain a middle class sensibility and lifestyle. I realise the authorial voice I use can be quite telling but was hoping to emulate Austen in this style.

THE JANE AUSTEN
HEN WEEKEND

Clair Humphries

THE JANE AUSTEN HEN WEEKEND

※

Clair Humphries

It began with a blocked loo.

'How?' I asked, staring as the sinister-looking stream of water oozed out from under the bathroom door.

'How do you think?' Anna glared at Lucy. 'Someone's toilet-bothering brat stuffed too much paper down there, didn't they?'

'That's not fair!' Lucy clutched a gloved hand dramatically to her ample chest. Her Empireline frock was doing its best to withstand her womanly curves, but I could see why Keira Knightley proved such a popular choice for costume drama casting directors. Anything above a C cup was perilous and clearly put the stitching under intolerable strain.

'It bloody is fair. You and Oscar have been locked in there for an hour.'

'He's not well, I told you. He can't help that—'

'Why bring him then? Couldn't your mum look after him or something?'

'Oh, I can tell you don't have kids! What am I supposed to do – he's been up all night with the runs, crying his eyes out. I can't just abandon him for the weekend!'

'Um, could you try not to swear please, Anna?' Rachel interrupted, looking up from her well-thumbed guide book. 'Genteel ladies of the Regency period wouldn't use that kind of language. And 'toilet-bothering' doesn't really make sense. One's 'toilet' usually referred to getting dressed, or powdering your nose, that sort of thing—'

We all looked at Rachel; now wasn't the best time for a lecture on early nineteenth century linguistics. Water was spreading rapidly across the flag stoned floor, accompanied by a distinctly whiffy odour. Wisely, Anna chose to ignore her and pressed on.

'Dragging your child down here with the squits is hardly fair on us either, is it? Now the loo's out of action and we've probably all been infected with whatever vile bug he's carrying.'

'What was I supposed to do? Stay at home while you all have a lovely time as usual? Well, I'm sick of it!' Lucy's lip began to wobble. 'I haven't been anywhere for ages – mums never get the chance to dress up and play. I just wanted some fun for a change.'

'Fun?' Anna waved her fan accusingly in my direction. 'Remind me, will you – how exactly is this meant to be fun? I'm freezing in this stupid dress, there's no pub for miles around and my favourite shoes are about to be written off by raw sewage!'

She had a point. The toilet overflow was gathering momentum and, squealing like the girls that we were, we hurried back down the corridor, escaping the pool of evil-smelling goo. Not the ideal beginning to a Jane Austen-themed hen weekend, I had to admit. And, yes, maybe I should take some of the blame – it was my idea. I'd booked the venue, hired the costumes and (with the help of my year three class) cobbled together the props, determined everything would be perfect for my best friend Rachel: romantic novelist and bride-to-be, who was marrying her own real life Mr Darcy next Saturday. The premise was simple enough. Four friends, two days and one country house. So far, so civilised. What, dear reader, could go wrong?

We retired to the drawing room. With his bowel temporarily at rest, three-year-old Oscar was sleeping soundly in the nursery while we gathered around the card table to discuss our options.

'We could have a go with a plunger,' I suggested in my best primary-school-teacher-rallying-a-class-of-eight-year-olds voice.

'Have you got a plunger handy?' Anna asked.

'Well, no—'

'Even if you did, we're hardly dressed for a spot of plumbing, are we?' Lucy said, blinking back tears, her arms folded beneath her heaving bosom. I scowled at her; frankly, I was getting fed up with her emotional outpourings and quivering flesh.

'Alright – you decide what to do,' I told her. 'Seeing as it's your child who got us into this mess.'

'I don't know what to do!' Lucy wailed into an embroidered white lace handkerchief that I'd sourced (rather cleverly, I thought) from eBay. I couldn't deny she was right though; none of us were suitably attired for manual labour, plunger or no plunger. It had taken hours to transform ourselves into Regency belles, doing our best to look the part with our hair curled and pinned up on top of our heads and our cheeks pinched pink. I'd planned a weekend of wafting round in muslin gowns, not shovelling sewage.

'What would Jane Austen do?' Rachel wondered aloud.

'I know exactly what Jane would do,' Anna said, standing up. 'She'd get a man in.'

Unfortunately, men weren't cheap – not in this part of rural England anyway.

'Sixty-quid call out charge,' Anna announced ten minutes later, snapping her mobile shut. 'That's before he does anything. And he might not get here for an hour.'

'Great. What do we do in the meantime?' Lucy asked.

'It says here that whist was a popular choice for ladies of good breeding,' Rachel read excitedly from her book. 'Elizabeth Bennet attends a whist party in *Pride and Prejudice*, and it's mentioned in *Emma* and in *Mansfield Park*—'

'Excellent! Let's play whist.' I felt my spirits lift; I'd packed cards, along with some gothic-looking pewter candlesticks. We gathered around the rosewood table and I arranged the candles while Anna opened the cards. This was more like it, I thought with satisfaction. Female bonding, just as Jane would have wanted. Outside, the evening was drawing in; dusk had settled, casting long, low shadows across the oak-panelled room. A perfect time for cards by candlelight. We would eat soon, I decided. Crumpets and dainty little cakes, with tea served in white china cups.

'Who's got matches?' Anna said as she shuffled the cards.

'Matches?' I frowned. 'I thought you'd bring a lighter. You're the only one who smokes—'

'I've given up.'

'What?' Lucy shrieked with laughter. 'Don't be ridiculous. You smoke more than anyone I know. You can't give up.'

'Well I have, so shut it.' Anna regarded her coolly. 'The flip side is I'm permanently starving and liable to punch someone at any moment.'

This was enough to silence all of us, even Lucy. In the City bank where she worked, Anna's temper was legendary. She spent her working day doing complicated things with stocks and derivatives, an area I knew nothing about, except it seemed to involve her screaming down the phone at a succession of ex-public schoolboys who were foolish enough to think they could screw her over. None of them could.

'So, no matches then.' Reluctantly, I went to turn the light on. Of course the house had electricity – along with central heating, Wi-Fi access and all the other accoutrements people expected from a historic country house in the twenty-first century. It did rather spoil the mood though, I felt, as the intriguing shadows of the drawing room were exposed in the harsh glare of artificial light.

'How many cards am I dealing?' Anna asked as I joined them again.

'No idea. Rachel? What are the rules?'

'I don't know – I've never played whist before.'

'But you're the one with the guide book,' I reminded her. 'You're always in the library; you said you'd do the research.'

'I've done my best!' Rachel slammed her book shut. 'I have had a wedding to organise, you know. I've been really busy, sorting out the cars, the flowers, the dress…'

It was true. For months Rachel had been planning her big day, choreographing every moment as precisely as the plot in one of her slushy novels. That was her dream: to be the great romantic heroine, to live out the happy endings she created on paper for real. It wasn't much to ask – who doesn't want their wedding day to be special? And here I was, the chief bridesmaid, stressing her out on what should have been a lovely, indulgent weekend. I started to feel bad.

'Sorry, Rachel.' I put my gloved hand over hers. 'You just sit back and relax, we'll find something fun to do. How else did young Regency ladies amuse themselves?'

Lucy leaned over and picked up the guide book.

'Um, cross stitch—' she read aloud.

'Boring,' Anna said.

'Charades—'

'Not bloody likely.'

'Pianoforte recitals!' Lucy's eyes lit up. 'Oh, let's do that – there's a piano in the room next door and I love that bit in *Sense and Sensibility* where Marianne and Willoughby play together and he's watching her in that way – you know, all rakish and sort of brooding and repressed—'

'Please!' Anna rolled her eyes.

'Can anyone play the piano?' Rachel asked hopefully. I suddenly found all eyes on me.

'No,' I said firmly (and truthfully).

'But you're a schoolteacher,' Anna said.

'And?'

'All my teachers could play the piano.'

'And mine,' Lucy said.

'Mine too,' Rachel added.

'Well, good for them.' I shrugged. 'Because I can't, sorry.' Three collective sighs of disappointment echoed around the wood-panelled walls. Which was a bit rich, I thought – three years of teacher training had equipped me with a diverse range of skills: classroom management, extracting pencil rubbers from the ears of small children and the ability to construct lifelike models of dinosaurs to scale from bits of papier mache and Copydex. Mastering a musical instrument seemed to have been squeezed out of the modern Cert Ed curriculum. I explained this to my dear, loyal friends.

They remained unimpressed.

'All my teachers could play piano,' Anna reiterated, adding, 'no wonder kids can't read anymore and spend the whole time happy-slapping strangers in the street. Typical.' Before I could defend myself, she stood up. 'I'm going for a fag,' she said and swept grandly out of the drawing room.

Which left three of us.

'I'll go and check on Oscar,' Lucy said, getting to her feet. 'If he's still got a temperature I should really take him home – sorry, Rachel.' She looked apologetic. 'It's not very child-friendly here, is it? With the toilet and hygiene and everything—'

So then there were two.

Rachel started to sniffle. But all was not lost! I resolved then, dear reader, to save the day. I couldn't provide a rakish piano-playing suitor, an evening of sparkling yet genteel amusements or even a workable flushing loo for my party, but I had at my disposal something far, far superior. The one thing guaranteed to unite a group of females in even the direst of circumstances.

Cake.

I shouldn't have shouted at Lucy. It wasn't Oscar's fault that he'd gatecrashed our hen weekend, or blocked the toilet, or even that he'd managed (despite his upset stomach) to demolish the entire hamper of cupcakes in the half an hour we had faffed about in the drawing room. I know I should have held back – but it was the icing that did it. All those hours I'd spent, hunched over my kitchen table with the latest Nigella, anointing my home-made delicacies with chocolate sprinkles, little silver balls and edible flowers. I'd packed them so carefully too, along with my granny's best china and filigree napkins, a confection of girly delight that I knew would gain Rachel's approval and even that of Jane (God rest her soul) Austen herself. To find Oscar standing there, his grubby toddler mouth encrusted with pink icing was just too much.

'There's no need to be rude,' Lucy sobbed, smoothing his hair.

'Why shouldn't he be allowed a bit of cake?'

'A *bit* of cake? How much is left exactly, Rachel?'

Rachel peered into the depths of my ravaged wicker picnic hamper.

'None,' she replied. 'Apart from a few crumbs and some hundreds and thousands—'

'None!' I nearly exploded.

'He's not well!' Lucy yelled at me, as if that made it all better.

'We won't be having cake then,' Rachel said sadly and flipped the lid of the hamper shut.

'There's still crumpets,' I said. 'And I can make some tea—' but I knew that was it. The Jane Austen hen weekend ended here; I'd failed her. I was a rubbish chief bridesmaid, a rubbish event organiser and a thoroughly rubbish best friend.

Oscar emitted a loud burp.

'Mummy,' he said in that whiny toddler voice that reminded me why I'd chosen to teach eight-year-olds and not a nursery or foundation class. 'I think I do a sick now.'

My beautiful hamper. There was no time to explain politely (not that I was feeling especially polite at that point) to Lucy how priceless it was. Or why, as she thrust it beneath her retching child's chin, it might have been an idea to remove my granny's cherished Royal Doulton and napkins from it first. I could only watch, and whimper.

'Guess what?' Anna burst into the kitchen with a big grin on her face, trailing cigarette ash in her wake.

'What?' I asked weakly.

'The plumber's here and he's proper fit. Quick, come and look!'

We didn't need telling twice.

It is a truth universally acknowledged that all young ladies, when confronted by a single man in possession of a six-pack draped in a crisp, white, wet shirt, will inevitably swoon. The fact that the plumber's shirt was drenched in half a gallon of raw sewage could have taken the shine off it, but I was willing to overlook that, seeing as he was so handsome. And proper fit.

'Hi,' I said, watching as he wrestled with the waste pipe. 'Shouldn't you be wearing a boiler suit or something?'

'I was at my brother's wedding,' he said, looking up at me with deep brown eyes. 'But I came as soon as I could.'

'Thank you so much.' Our eyes remained locked. Despite this, I still managed to take in all the necessary details: the moody, furrowed brow beneath tousled dark hair, the fixed, firm jaw and the arm muscles that tensed impressively as he did something manly and complicated with a monkey wrench. I could have stood there in that bathroom all evening, oblivious to the sodden floor and heinous smell, if it meant spending more time with this Colin Firth-alike. Until Anna coughed and broke the reverie, reminding me that we had an audience. She stood in the doorway, smirking, along with Lucy, Rachel and Oscar who had thankfully stopped retching but nevertheless was still seriously cramping my style.

'Er, did you want a cup of tea?' I asked our hero, attempting to sound in control.

'No, I'm fine. But I could do with changing this shirt—' and the three of us ladies watched open-mouthed as he loosened the buttons.

'Oh, please do,' I said boldly – well, I was responsible for this weekend, wasn't I? It was only right to take charge. And it hadn't been a complete disaster, I reasoned, helping him out of his wet things. I wasn't such a bad chief bridesmaid after all. In fact, I had a feeling this weekend was about to get a whole lot better.

And I'm sure Jane would have approved.

❦

My inspiration: Mr Darcy and a blocked toilet. A recent sewage leak in my house inspired me, alongside my love of Jane Austen's novels and happy endings.

ONE CHARACTER IN SEARCH OF HER LOVE STORY ROLE

Felicity Cowie

ONE CHARACTER IN SEARCH OF HER
LOVE STORY ROLE

❧

Felicity Cowie

Hannah Peel was dispatched by her author to shadow heroines from *Pride and Prejudice* and *Jane Eyre*.[1] Like all CAST cardholders, Hannah was well aware of the Intertextuality Act which had come in around the start of the twentieth century, acknowledging that writers could make use of existing characters, consciously or otherwise. Hannah hoped to use her shadowing work to convince her author that she could take a larger role. While some characters might be comfortable to turn in some very slight work and be used solely to comment on the downfall of the hero, Hannah was not one of them. She suspected her author of being inexperienced. Frequently, Hannah wished she might be

---

1   The work experience referred to here was arranged by the Characters' Affiliation for Shadowing and Training (CAST). The origins of CAST are uncertain but it is known to have operated internationally for several thousand years, offering support to millions of hard-working fictional characters.
　　Flann O'Brien refers to CAST on p25 of his novel, At Swim-Two-Birds (London: Penguin, 1939) He writes, 'Characters should be interchangeable as between one book and another. The entire corpus of existing literature should be regarded as a limbo from which discerning authors could draw their characters as required. The modern novel should be largely a work of reference. Most authors spend their time saying what has been said before – usually said much better. A wealth of references to existing works would acquaint the reader instantly with the nature of each character.'

commissioned to work with Ali Smith or Shirley Hazzard or Kazuo Ishiguro, but that was unfair. Every author deserved at least a chance to listen to their characters.

When Hannah arrived at the Netherfield Ball she immediately noted that Mr Bingley was dancing with an Unnamed Character at the far side of the floor. Hannah approached Jane Bennet, who was sitting apart, struggling with a word puzzle.

'Miss Bennet? I'm Hannah Peel. I'm going to be the chief female character in a modern novel. I've been sent here, by CAST, to shadow you.'

Miss Bennet put the puzzle book aside and stood.

'You are most welcome to Netherfield, Miss Peel. But I am afraid you have mistaken me for my sister, Miss Elizabeth Bennet. It is she who is the heroine of this novel. I am *Jane* Bennet and a secondary character in a parallel subplot. Shall I take you to her?'

Hannah studied a print-out of her CAST email.

'No, it says here that my placement is with you. After that I'm off to Thornfield Hall to shadow another Jane.'

'Oh,' said Miss Bennet, her face flushing with pleasure, 'Miss Eyre! You are to visit Miss Eyre? Please pass on my warmest regards to her. And to Miss Helen Burns if you should be travelling with Miss Eyre through her Lowood years. They both came to work with me when they were in development. They studied my equanimity.'

She gestured to the couch and she and Hannah sat down together.

'Miss Eyre split her placement between myself and dear Lizzy. She shared Lizzy's desire to argue for the rights of a lower class character to hold and express feelings. Miss Eyre studied Lizzy's confrontations with Lady Catherine and Mr Darcy before making her passionate speeches to Mrs Reed and Mr Rochester.

'In fact,' said Miss Bennet, lowering her steady voice, 'Miss Eyre came here at first of her own will. For you know that her author was most unhappy with Miss Austen?'[2]

Laughter exploded from the side of the dance floor. Hannah turned to see a man and woman unsuccessfully attempting to compose themselves, doubling up with further laughter whenever they looked up at one another.

'Who is that?' asked Hannah.

'That is dearest Lizzy and Mr Darcy. They are no doubt attempting their scene where Mr Darcy refers to her as "tolerable" which they both find most amusing.'

'Mr Darcy!' exclaimed Hannah.

'You have already made the acquaintance of Mr Darcy?' asked Miss Bennet very politely.

'Oh no,' said Hannah, 'but a lot of my friends have worked with him. He's a very popular hero just now, after the Andrew Davies adaptation of *Pride and Prejudice* in 1995 and the subsequent Bridget Jones novels. Oh, Miss Bennet, what's wrong?'

Miss Bennet had started to frown.

'It is nothing, Miss Peel, only that my poor Mr Bingley suffers a little for Mr Darcy's popularity. CAST does not have so much work for Mr Bingley.'

'But Mr Darcy is every woman's ideal man, Jane. Aren't you secretly disappointed that you don't end up with him?'

Miss Bennet shook her head firmly.

'Mr Bingley singles me out from the start of our acquaintance

2   Miss Bennet refers to Charlotte Bronte's documented antipathy to Jane Austen. An example of this can be found in Bronte's letter of 12 April, 1850 to W. S. Williams where she writes, 'She [Austen] ruffles her reader by nothing vehement, disturbs him by nothing profound: the Passions are perfectly unknown to her.' However, an explanation as to why Bronte grudgingly allowed Jane Eyre to continue her CAST placement with Miss Bennet may be found in an earlier letter of 12 January, 1848 to George Lewes in which she writes, 'Miss Austen is only shrewd and observant.'

and, as soon as he is sensible of my returned feelings, he proposes marriage to me. But I am not sure that Mr Darcy is always so good a man until Lizzy speaks to him of his improper pride.'

Hannah considered this and said, 'Maybe that's why Mr Darcy is always getting shadowed? Because he gets his act together after Lizzy gives him what for? Gives women authors and readers some belief that they can turn their men about, doesn't it? But Bingley's already an all-round decent bloke from the start.'

Miss Bennet laughed and asked, 'What do you need to learn from me, Miss Peel?'

'Well, like you I'm very attractive and good but, at the moment, stuff sort of just happens to me. My bloke loves me from the start. He proposes and we get married. I get scouted as a model but, I dunno, I don't like it much. I feel just like a coat hanger. I want to have a baby but I'm not sure I get the chance in the novel to tell my husband about what I really want from him.'

Miss Bennet nodded quickly, 'Yes, if Charlotte Lucas had spoken to me, as she does to Lizzy, of the need for me to make my feelings for Mr Bingley plainer, then I do not believe it would have been so easy for others to convince him of my indifference. And we would have wed within the first quarter of the novel—'

'Miss Bennett, would you mind if I take notes?' asked Hannah who now sat poised over a notebook with pen.

'Shall I speak slowly for you, Miss Peel?'

'It's okay. My bloke, Bill, is a super-duper journalist and he's been teaching me shorthand when our author's been asleep. So I should be able to keep up. I've already got up to 100 words a minute.'

Miss Bennet continued, 'It is Mr Darcy who returns Bingley to me after conveying my true feelings for him. And Mr Darcy has them from dear Lizzy. So my happiness rises and falls with Mr

Darcy's perceptions of my character. That is rather hard. But I am very blessed at the end of the novel, securing not just my own happiness but also that of my dear family. For you know that until Lizzy and I marry so happily, there is an entail which hangs over us all? My father's death would have left Mama and my sisters in difficult circumstances if we had married otherwise. Does your marriage please your family?'

'Yes. Like your mum with Bingley, my mum is quick to invite my bloke into our house. He's only 15 and a runaway when we all meet so he lives with me and my parents. He's not like Bingley because when he turns up he's dirt poor, but he's got brains and earning potential. My parents don't care much about the cash. But we're a close family. They like having Bill grow up under the same roof as me. They believe it'll be a safe way for me to fall in love.'

Miss Bennet sighed and said, 'Your parents are perhaps more sensible than my dear father to family responsibilities. I am afraid he learns a very hard lesson when Lydia elopes with Wickham after he fails to heed or check her nature. She is but 15 when she meets Wickham and lacking the prudence brought about by living within loving constraints.'

Suddenly, Miss Bennet smiled, 'Miss Peel, is your man to come and shadow Mr Bingley?'

Hannah shook her head, 'I'm afraid not, Jane. My fella turns out to be rather messed up.'

Miss Bennet said, 'And so that is why you are to go to Thornfield Hall? To shadow Miss Eyre and her poor Mr Rochester?'

When Hannah arrived at Thornfield Hall, Jane Eyre was away from home. Mrs Fairfax invited her into a small, snug room.

'That's Grace Poole,' said Mrs Fairfax gesturing towards a

woman sitting at a round table by the fireplace, rapidly shuffling a pack of cards.

'Do you play, Miss—?'

'Peel,' said Hannah, 'I'm Hannah Peel, here to shadow Jane Eyre.'

'And this is Bertha.'

A tall, sad woman turned from the fire, which she stirred with a poker. She extended a nail-bitten hand to Hannah and said, 'Welcome to Thornfield. How long are you to stay with us here?' [3]

An alarm sounded.

'Goodness, that startled me!' exclaimed Bertha Antoinette, 'Come on, Miss Peel. It's another fire alarm.'

The characters exited the house and waited in the drive for the siren to stop. Adele, Sophie and Leah were already outside. Grace Poole smoked a cigarette and Adele skipped around them all, breathlessly singing '*Sur le pont d'Avignon*'.

'Is it a real fire?' asked Hannah.

'I doubt it, Miss Peel,' said Mrs Fairfax, 'it is most likely a test. Mr Rochester thought it best to put in a system so that none of us gets hurt.'[4]

---

3   Before anyone contacts the CAST hotline to report Bertha for contravening the Acting Out Of Character Act, it is essential to remember that Bertha is of course Bertha *Antoinette* of Rhys vs Cosway Mason Rochester. It took 27 years of legal dispute between author Jean Rhys and CAST, before *Wide Sargasso Sea* could be made public. And of those 27 years, it took Rhys the final nine to gain Bertha Antoinette's full cooperation. Francis Wyndham refers to this on p10 of her introduction to *Wide Sargasso Sea* (London: Penguin, 1966): 'For many years, Jean Rhys has been haunted by the figure of the first Mrs Rochester – the mad wife in *Jane Eyre*. The present novel – completed at last after much revision and agonised rejection of earlier versions – is her story.'

4   All members of the Characters' Affiliation live in the 'continuous present'. This state is explained by Mother on p63 of Luigi Pirandello's *Six Characters in Search of an Author* when she says, 'No, it's happening now, it's happening all the time! My torment isn't over. I am alive and constantly present at every moment of my agony, which keeps coming back, alive and constantly present.' (Translated by Stephen Mulrine, London: Nick Hern Books, 2003)

     Mr Rochester installed a robust fire safety system at Thornfield Hall in order to safeguard the characters from any fire-related injuries, excepting those demanded by the plot.

At that moment—[5]

At that moment, a slight figure, gripped by a stocky, pugnacious man, could be seen approaching the house from the direction of the chapel.

'Good God! Miss Eyre's back from the doomed wedding already with Edward. I must return to the third storey,' exclaimed Bertha Antoinette. She started to rip at her clothes and pulled her black hair into disarray as she ran back into the house. The fire alarm stopped. Grace Poole hastily stamped out her cigarette and followed her.

Mrs Fairfax said to Hannah, 'In eight minutes, Miss Eyre will withdraw to her own room. You may be able to speak with her briefly until Mr Rochester arrives. He will sit outside her door before he makes his inappropriate offer of sinful living.'

Hannah knocked on Miss Eyre's door.

'Ed?' exclaimed a voice in surprise.

---

5   I'm sorry to interrupt again with another footnote but I thought perhaps it was only fair to give the characters' side of the Pirandello Uprisings as I did bring up Pirandello in the previous footnote.

      This unhappy affair is a very rare instance of insurrection amongst the Characters' Affiliation. Although characters are, of course, used to working with mentally unstable authors and usually deal with them with consummate professionalism, the Pirandello Six, as they came to be known, accused the playwright of characterism. The characters felt that even the very title of the play implied that characters have no lives of their own except those given validation by authors.

      The Pirandello Six protested by intentionally making themselves unknowable. This is described by the play's first director, Dario Niccodemi, in his memoir *Tempo Passato* (Milan: Treves, 1929, pp 82-3): 'The actors were still somewhat lost. They were unable to form an opinion about what they were saying. And this just cannot be. An actor without an opinion about the work he's performing in is like a lamp that has gone out.'

      Pirandello further angered the characters by insisting that the struggling actors 'must no longer be actors but the very characters of the play they are performing in'. (ibid. p87)

      The Pirandello Six felt that this command threatened the autonomy of fictional civilians.

      The result of this stand-off is described by Jennifer Lorch in *Six Characters in Search of an Author: Plays in Production* (Cambridge: Cambridge University Press, 2005, p.31): 'The reaction to the first night of *Six Characters in Search of an Author* has made of it a theatrical legend: scuffles in the theatre and a hasty exit by Pirandello and his daughter by the stage door thence to be bundled into a taxi by friends.'

      Anyway, back to Thornfield Hall...

Hannah entered, 'No, it's me, Hannah Peel. I've come on a CAST placement. I know it's not a great time but—'

'Come in, Miss Peel. I thought it strange that Ed should be knocking at the door. I usually stumble over him sitting in a chair across my threshold, some time in the afternoon.'

'Have I disturbed you getting undressed?' asked Hannah, who saw a square, blond veil on the bed.

'I need to take off my gown mechanically and put on my stuff dress from yesterday. But I have all morning to do that. Miss Peel, are you certain that you are to shadow me?'

'Yes,' said Hannah.

'But you are very beautiful. Even more magnificent than Miss Ingram. And I am small and plain.'

'What! Are you kidding me? Your look is so right now. Slight, boyish figure, elfin. You might even be a size zero. And your skin is clear, hair in great condition and a versatile style. As for height, Kate Moss is five seven. Victoria Beckham and Cheryl Cole are way shorter than that.'

'Miss Peel! How can this be true?' asked Miss Eyre, moving to a very small mirror to study her face, 'And I'm so much used to being plain,' she said, wonderingly.

'Jane, you are hot right now.'

'Hot?' repeated Miss Eyre.

'Still—' said Hannah.

'What?'

'Well, it is all a bit of a waste of time, isn't it? Looks come and go, don't they? But it's your actions which count, isn't it, Jane? Miss Eyre?'

Miss Eyre continued to consider her small face in the mirror.

'Miss Eyre?'

'When you said "hot" just a moment ago, Miss Peel, I wonder if you were teasing me as I am so very plain, am I not?'

Hannah sat down in a chair and said, 'Look, Miss Eyre, you

must know you've got something going on, otherwise how do you explain all of your marriage proposals, right, left and centre.'

'There are not so many. Two.'

'Right, one from Rochester who's minted and chased by women, and another from St John who's attractive and ambitious. Between them you're holding the whole deck. You ain't doing badly.'

'Yes, but sometimes I do wonder if it is my littleness which attracts them. After all, it is not so very hard to destroy something small when you are finished using it. I have no family in the world to protect me, for most of the novel anyway, and I wonder if, knowing that and in desperate want of a mate, Mr Rochester proposed this impossible wedding to me. When he asks me to travel abroad with him, unmarried, that cannot be with any true mindfulness of my long-term welfare. And St John plainly does not love me but presses me to travel to India with him where it is almost certain that we shall perish in the difficult climate. He asks me to give him my life. I wonder if life might be more ordered if I were to train myself out of my strongest feelings. But then, I suppose I do not really wish for a passionless life.'

Miss Eyre sighed and lowered herself onto the bed.

'Are you ever tempted to marry St John, Miss Eyre? I ask you because when my husband Bill suffers and pushes me away, my friend Flash asks me to start a relationship with him. I don't know what to do. Bill is very hard work, like Mr Rochester. But I love him. I want to have a baby and Flash offers me that. But I don't love Flash. It feels morally wrong to have a child with someone you don't love.'

'I do not wish to marry St John, Miss Peel, because he does not love me. God did not give me my life to throw away on any fruitless mission. Nor you. Nor any character. Regardless of what Mr Pirandello may write on the subject.'

Hannah, emboldened by Miss Eyre's passion and disgusted with the objectification of Miss Bennet returned to the CAST HQ in a resolute mood. She showed her card at the barriers to pass.[6]

She filed her report back to her author and hoped that the equipment wasn't playing up and that her author could hear her distinct voice.

❦

My inspiration: In the early stages of writing my novel, I felt uncertain about my central female character, Hannah Peel. I wondered if I might get to know her better by having her interact with other literary heroines. I have studied *Pride and Prejudice* five times (from GCSE to an MA in Creative Writing at Bath Spa). My admiration for this novel influences the way I draw characters. My own novel is quite dark and it was a joy to write this 'essay' for a complete change. It worked, too. It gave me Hannah's voice.

6　The barriers were erected following the rise of the docu-drama genre on television. Many 'characters' from docu-dramas, including *Crimewatch* 're-enactment characters', wished to be admitted to CAST. When they were refused membership they stormed the headquarters and burst into the main Story Room, hurling about computers, printers and microphones, which accredited CAST members were attempting to use to file back their stories to their authors. Several days of hand-to-hand combat between CAST members and their non-CAST member brothers (sisters and multiple other family relations) followed. Destruction was so widespread and costly that the CAST funding for the modernisation of the aging communication system had to be spent instead on rehousing the headquarters in Portacabins. The impact of all of this on the quality of communication lines between characters and their authors is detailed by A. S. Byatt: 'It was as if the novel was already written, floating in the air on a network of electrons. I could hear it talking to itself. I sensed that if I would but sit and listen, it would come through, all ready.'

SECOND FRUITS

Stephanie Tillotson

SECOND FRUITS

❧

Stephanie Tillotson

Rosamunde Shaw neatly folded together the pink pages of the *Financial Times* and, finding little consolation there, asked herself, 'Now, I wonder how all this will end?'

Her gaze slid cleanly down from the thickening autumn clouds above her to the glass and black wall of the building opposite, down to the wet London pavements thirty-two storeys below. In the offices around her own, the flames of fluorescent light were catching, running along the ledges and leaping from atom to atom in the recycled, dry oxygen of the city air. Now that the bank had failed she wondered if they would see people jumping from these windows, as they had done in Wall Street after 1929. What determination had resolved that leap into oblivion, was it simply the fear of something yet worse to come?

Guto had told her, on the first day they met, about a play he'd seen, the tale of a Welsh queen who, in middle age, had taken a young lover with passionate, unquenchable fervour. When the King had discovered her betrayal, he had ordered that the lover be hanged outside the Queen's chamber window, where she could heed the hammering and the intensity of the execution drums.

'That's a horrible story. Why did you tell me that?' Rosamunde had demanded.

.'They didn't hang him,' replied Guto earnestly, his mouth almost touching her face so that she could hear him above the sound of the waves and the wailing of the boat's engine. 'With the noose around his neck, the Queen's lover jumped from the scaffold to his death. Don't you think that is wonderful, Rosa? What courage! What defiance!'

She hadn't understood but she had enjoyed the feel of his breath on her face. She thought it might just be despair that had caused the lover to jump but she hadn't understood Guto then, after all she was only sixteen. It was August and her newly received exam results had been even better than predicted. For once her father had seemed pleased, pleased enough to allow her to join a small party of girls from school, boarding the day ferry from Penarth pier to Ilfracombe bay and back again. What he didn't know was that Amelia Edwards had invited her brother and some of his friends to come along and that Amelia's brother had brought several bottles of wine with him. Guto was one of the brother's friends and, an hour or so into the trip, when the cliffs around Cardiff and Barry were little more than a charcoal smudge on the horizon, he had brought over a cup of red wine. Rosamunde did not drink it, though she had sipped it once. At Ilfracombe they had eaten light-brown scones with sweet strawberry jam and sticky cream. Later, as they stood on the beach, he had tried to kiss her. She had decided that she liked this, though she was nervous of what else he might try to do. Amelia said a boy had pushed his hand down the front of her knickers and put his finger inside her but Guto had never once done that to Rosa. Now she wondered what it would have felt like if he had.

She turned from the window back to the television in the corner above the filing cabinet. There had been a time when she only switched on the set to check the market prices. Tonight she was watching the early evening news. She could see a young man on the screen, someone with whom it seemed she had worked. He was crossing the crowded concourse in front of the building, a cardboard box in his hands. The dark jacket of his suit stirred as he walked, his rounded shoulders taking the weight of the box. A voice stumbled on, a voice unable to hide its excitement at the latest catastrophic news from the bank. Thirty-two storeys above the now empty concourse, Rosamunde watched the young man leaving the building, walking towards the Underground.

Her father had not approved of Guto. Because of the way his Welsh name is pronounced (the 'u' sounding like an 'i' to her father's ears), he was always referred to as 'the little git'. But then Guto's father had not been pleased by his son's growing attachment to a girl who only spoke English. Guto's parents had both been teachers of Welsh and had brought up their children to be proud of their otherness. Guto's dad now worked for the Examining Board and Guto's mum was the headteacher at the comprehensive school he attended, where he was taught through a mysterious language Rosa had only ever heard on the television. He told her stories from books she had not known existed and learned of a history that seemed to have almost nothing to do with Shakespeare or English kings and queens. And all this in a building only twenty minutes walk away from her own school, where she was expected to devote herself to the development of her natural talents for Mathematics, Latin and Lacrosse.

'Why did your Dad send you to that snobby girls' school?' Guto had asked.

'It was when Mrs Shaw ran back home to her mammy,' she had replied.

'You see,' he had laughed, 'It's just not normal!'

'Aberystwyth University,' her father had sneered in exasperation. 'What the hell does he want to go there for?'

'To study Welsh Literature.'

'And what will he be able to do with that? He'll be fit for nothing but teaching if he's not careful and teachers earn a pittance. That boy of yours has no ambition.' In her father's eyes not to have any ambition was the worst failing possible. He had never spoken of courage or defiance with admiration, not to her anyway, yet how much he had displayed as the cancer threatened to overwhelm his failing flesh. It had been no more unnatural than the tide going out but Rosa's father had clawed and hammered against it every minute of every day, steadfastly refusing to die in peace. The hospice had rung her late one Monday afternoon somewhere in the middle of this surprising month. 'Come now,' the doctor had advised and an hour later she was running down the platform at Paddington Station, cursing her short legs and her expanding waistline, leaping for the door just as the whistle blew on the train to Cardiff Central. All night long she sat by her father's bed watching his chest expand and contract. She had remembered the prayers her mother's religion had taught her, even though her father had nothing but contempt for 'frail subservience and ignorance'.

'Not in my house,' he had shouted, 'you will not teach my children the ways of fawning and toadying.'

'Your father is a bad man, Rosamunde.' Her mother had stood her ground and, when he had forgotten to collect her from the hospital after the birth of Rosamunde's little brother, had taken the next taxi to the airport and gone home to her own mother in Tipperary. Thereafter Rosa's father only referred to his wife as 'Mrs Shaw', who continued to stand her ground and would not entertain the idea of divorce until Rosamunde was forwarded to her mother in Ireland. In response, her father had taken Rosa out of the convent primary and made her sit the entrance exam to an exclusive girls' school in Cardiff. She had passed easily, so her father's next move was to buy a two-bedroomed luxury flat on the cliffs above the sea in posh Penarth. Suddenly their neighbours were judges, barristers and wealthy businessmen and her friends at school were the daughters of judges, barristers and wealthy businessmen. There had never been any further talk of divorce.

'Do you think he knows that I am here?' Rosamunde had asked the nurse.

'He can probably hear you. Why don't you talk to him?'

'I'm still here, Daddy,' she had told him time and time again through that night, her hand around his. 'Pray for us sinners, now and at the hour of our death,' she murmured as his chest contracted. This time the breath did not shudder out, his body remained silent and still. 'Has he gone?' she asked. The nurse took a step towards the bed as his body rippled and reached out for life once again.

'Listen to this, Rosa.' They sat together on the sea wall, the sun shining on the last days they shared before Guto went away to university. He had made her promise she would come and see him but her father later steadfastly refused to let her leave the flat now that her A level exams were in sight. 'You've got far too much work to do,' he'd said and Guto had grown resentful of taking the bus to Cardiff and then being forbidden to see her. So Rosa's father achieved his heart's delight. He was able to stand in wine bars, an empty glass in his hand, boasting of his daughter who was studying Law at Oxford.

'Listen to this, Rosa,' side by side on the sea wall at Penarth, Guto with a book in his hand. 'It says here that the greatest mystery in the world is that man is mortal and yet greets every day as though he were immortal. That can't be right,' he'd said jumping from the wall and holding out his hand, inviting her to follow him. 'We're not that important. What do you think is the greatest mystery, lovely Rosamunde?' He caught her as she slid down onto the beach.

'A volcano,' she had replied, 'the most beautiful, terrifying, wonderful thing on earth.'

He grinned mischievously. 'Did you know,' he draped his arm casually across her shoulders, 'in Nicaragua, to appease the god of fire, only the most beautiful virgins were sacrificed to the boiling lava lake of Masaya Volcano?' His other arm was catching her across the backs of her knees so that she was powerless to stop him lifting her above the shallow waves. 'How would you have liked that?' he asked and then let her drop into the water, standing above her laughing.

It was in the last few minutes before dawn that Rosamunde's father had stopped breathing. She waited for the returning spasm but this time it had not come again. Afterwards she sat with him for an hour. There had been more tea and, suddenly, there were biscuits. He was exactly as he had always looked but she would not touch him again, afraid that he had already grown colder and that this would be her last memory of him; afraid that, in her subsequent dreams of him, she would reach out and he would be like stone. Across his cheeks, steel grey tips had begun to appear, 'You need a shave, Dad,' she said and walked away.

'It's not fair!' she shouted, as she stood in the car park trying to call a taxi. 'People don't die at sixty-four.' In Rosamunde's hand her mobile phone began to scream. Automatically she answered it, though she recognised the number.

'Thank Christ, Ros! Where the hell are you?'

'Cardiff.'

'Well get the next pony and trap back here immediately, the Bank's about to go tits up!' Her angry boss disconnected. A synthetic bubble of water rose and floated vertically over the screen.

She did not go back to London that day but stayed and registered her father's death. Kieran Shaw, born Dublin, 1943, died Cardiff, 15 September 2008. She signed it, Rosamunde Shaw, daughter, present at the death. When she returned to work her boss had told her how sorry he was to have disturbed her at such a sad time and then he had sobbed dryly for his annual bonus: 'I earned that money, I deserve it.' But they both knew that no one was going to step up to the plate and save this moribund bank.

Now, an empty cardboard box on her desk, Rosamunde tried to sweep away the final meal of bread, brie and apple from the crevices in her computer keyboard and then switched off the television. In the end she left the box, taking only the fountain pen her father had given her on the day her mother went. There were no family photographs anyway, only a novel she had half read and no longer cared for. Tomorrow she would put her London house on the market and, once again, take the train from Paddington back to Cardiff. There she would carry her father's ashes down to Penarth pier, to the exact splinter of wood where, twenty-one years before, on the very day she had left school, she had stood in her summer gingham dress and blazer and thrown her straw hat into the sea. She had watched as it nudged and shrugged across the gentle undulations until she grew tired of waiting for it to drown.

It would be different this time. She knew that what was left of her father, sealed in his expensive urn, would not float but be gulped up and sink to the bottom of the bay. Then she would move into his flat, book a ticket to Sicily and, she promised herself, however demanding the climb, she would find the tenacity to make the four-day trek up the volatile slopes of Mount Etna.

Rosamunde and the month of October had settled into her father's flat when, sitting in a café opposite the travel agent's, comparing prices in holiday brochures for Italy, she looked up to see Guto's mother crossing the floor.

'I read about your father in the local paper. I am so sorry.'

'Thank you,' she replied.

'Would you mind if I told Guto?' his mother asked.

'Of course not. How is he?'

He had done well, rising to a senior rank among the civil servants at the Welsh Assembly Government. A respected and trusted translator, he had worked at the UN as well as in Cardiff and London. 'In London?' Rosamunde interrupted.

'He often asks after you,' Guto's mother buttoned her coat to leave and then, as if changing her mind, she leant forward over the plastic table. 'I know he was only a boy but he nearly broke his young heart over you.'

A postcard dropped onto her father's doormat the following morning. The photograph was of a sandy sweep of bay and the Irish Sea stretching flat out to Cardigan Island. On the back he had written:

Dearest Rosa – Mum has just rung to tell me about your dad. I am so sorry and hope you know that I am thinking of you at this miserable time. Over is the view from my garden. After my divorce came through I decided to buy some land out here. I am now working for the Welsh Pony and Cob Society and am hoping to do some breeding myself in the next year or so. Come anytime – we could walk and ride or just sit by the sea and drink some red wine. My love, as always, Guto.

My inspiration: The inspiration for my story comes from the themes and characters in *Persuasion*. Beginning with the single image of Louisa Musgrove's jump from the Cobb at Lyme Regis, I attempted a contemporary retelling of Anne Elliot and Captain Wentworth's experience of separation, maturation and second chance.

THE SCHOOL TRIP

Jacqui Hazell

THE SCHOOL TRIP

❧

Jacqui Hazell

Stop. I have to stop.

Wheezing like an idiot.

Where's my inhaler?

My bag's stuffed: packed lunch, Diet Coke, project folder, mobile, Tampax, I can't find it. Why can I never find it? They should make them fluorescent.

'Sorry,' I'm in the way – doorway to Victory News – better move. Oh, it's the Jolly Jack Tar – violent dump – thank God it's shut.

That's it, there it is.

Okay, breathe out loads. Now puff, and puff again.

Embarrassing and never works fast enough.

Wish I could wait a while, but I have to run, Mr Sole will be doing his nut.

Breathe slowly, or should that be deeply? Be calm. It's stress-related, according to Mum. She should know seeing as she causes it all.

Okay, Johnsons Shoes, Mothercare, Debenhams, the concrete fountain, Top Shop – wish I could look but I can't – oh, slow down.

Bag strap is killing me. Nelson's café and the pound shop – can't see that nice bloke, must be his day off.

Wait, catch breath, I need to cross.

There's the coach by the main gate.

It's the usual English mustard turd of a bus, it matches the school. If you did one of those quizzes like you get in Minx Magazine, you know where you have to match the celebrity to the dog: Paris Hilton and her chihuahua, Sharon Osborne and her pug and Lily Allen and her English bull terrier. Well, the school equivalent would be Portsmouth High for Girls teamed with a gleaming, silver coach with onboard toilet facilities, seatbelts and headrests with inbuilt DVD players and this turd-mobile teamed with my school, Portsmouth City Comp. The dumping ground for hopeless cases and kids whose parents never bothered to fight tooth and nail to get them in anywhere decent.

It's an eight-storey, 70s block with a few other flat-roofed buildings branching off at right angles, an eyesore, and to make it worse they've painted all the window frames a dark, dismal seaweed green like the crappy uniform. It's listed of course, but that's Portsmouth for you, so bombed out during the war, they struggle to find anything worth listing.

I can see Mr Sole beside the bus in his stripy knitwear and slacks.

'Imperative, Lucy Welch, what does imperative mean?' He's shouting at me, going on about the last thing he said the day before. 'It's imperative you all get to school on time tomorrow.'

'I'm sorry, sir, I'm having the worst day.' Did he hear me wheeze? I'm trying to hide it, but I'm really hot and probably red, not to mention sweaty.

'You can tell me all about it in detention tomorrow, Lucy.'

Mathew Relf is at the front. He's holding up his fingers in an 'L' shape by his forehead. 'Loser,' he says, and Eric Boulter sniggers.

The words 'Shut it, volcano face' are on the tip of my tongue when I notice his mum seated opposite, talking to Kelvin's mum. Both women glance over.

They're talking about me or more likely my mum, I know it.

'Find a seat quickly, Lucy, you've held us up long enough.'

Megan is already sitting next to Katie. She mouths 'sorry' to me and shrugs. I've got to sit next to Janine and I haven't even brought my iPod.

'All right, Janine,' I say, sitting down on the brown-flecked upholstery.

'All right,' she says, beaming at me, 'have you heard the new Lady Ga Ga?'

'Quieten down, everyone,' says Mr Sole, 'just a few words before we go. No chewing gum, no mobiles, no fizzy drinks. It's going to take a good hour to get there then there'll be a short talk and a tour of the house, followed by lunch and then back to school in time for the bell. Does anyone have any questions?' Mr Sole looks towards the back of the bus. 'Yes, Akshat.'

'I get travel sick.'

A few people moan.

'I suggest you come forward and sit at the front.'

Akshat moves up the bus, knocking everyone with his oversized sports bag.

'Cretin,' says Katie.

The bus moves off with a shudder and the clunking of gears.

'It's like a right boring place to go, innit,' says Janine. 'My cousin's school went to Chessington World of Adventures. They went on Rameses' Revenge and the Rattlesnake and everything.'

'I'm gonna have a nap, Janine. I didn't get much sleep last night.'

'Why's that, Loos?'

'Dunno really, just couldn't sleep.'

As if I'd tell her how it all kicked off once I got back from swimming. I wouldn't tell her anything.

'You don't look tired,' she studies me with her hard brown eyes. 'You look nice, you always look nice, and your hair's so pretty,' she fiddles with the bit that's hanging down my shoulder. 'I wish I had blonde hair like yours. You're so lucky.'

'Janine, I really need to sleep,' I shut my eyes, and concentrate on breathing. It's almost back to normal, while the inside of my eyelids are all red and squiggly as if my head's on fire. It is. Perhaps I should listen to Janine go on about theme parks and pop stars. It would take my mind off things.

Diaries are dangerous, I knew that, though I thought the risk was all mine, like if Amy found out who I fancy or who I'd kissed.

I'm kicking myself. Normally, I'm so careful. You have to be when you share a room. I never write in front of Amy. I wait till she's out or in the bathroom or else I take it with me. And then, when I am writing, cross-legged on my bed, I always have a cushion close by so I can hide it. I reckon I'll always have a few seconds once I hear the door.

Mind you, I didn't hear the phone at first. I must have been too engrossed. Then Dad was shouting up the stairs and I know not to ignore Dad if he shouts. Still, Amy should never have read it. And she certainly shouldn't have told Dad.

'Lucy, are you crying?'

Oh God, Janine's curly head is hovering right over me.

'It's nothing, the sun's in my eyes.'

Janine gives me the kind of hard look I'd normally run from if I didn't already know how much she admires me.

'It's just the sun, I just woke up. I'm all right now. What were you saying about Lady Ga Ga?'

*

After about an hour the coach leaves the motorway and trundles along a few quaint country roads where the period houses are all absurdly pretty with perfect, flower-filled gardens and not a hint of dark green woodwork anywhere.

'Looks like a film set, doesn't it,' I say.

'People really live here, yeah?' says Janine.

The boys at the front start to cheer and whoop.

'That was the coach park,' shouts Kelvin, 'He's missed it.'

Mr Sole jumps up to peer out of the side of the bus then has a quick word with the driver.

'He has bloody missed it,' I say to Janine.

Next thing we know, he's trying to do a three-point turn in a tiny country road and backs into what is probably a listed Elizabethan wall resulting in more cheers from the boys. The bus stops. The driver gets out, inspects back of bus and glances at wall. Wall looks okay, don't know about bus.

He gets back in, manages to manoeuvre it into the right direction, finds the coach park and at last we can all get out.

Mr Sole has this strange, mesmerised expression. 'That's it, that's where she lived,' he says, looking across the road at a neat, red-brick, rectangular house with white-framed picture windows and a green sweep of garden on the corner with a majestic, ancient tree.

'It's beautiful,' I say. 'Here, sir, I thought you said she didn't have much money.'

'She didn't, it was her brother who looked after her.'

'Give me MTV Cribs any day,' says Janine, making hip hop gangster-style gestures with her hands. 'I like penthouses with walls of glass.'

Where the hell is Megan?

Behind me, thank God.

'How's your head?' she smiles.

'What?'

'Janine – is she doing your head in?'

'You have no idea.'

Mr Sole leads the way to an outbuilding that's been converted into a classroom. It's a pleasant, light, whitewashed room with chairs and there's a young woman with long dark hair and a trendy fringe, dressed in a white linen blouse and trousers. 'Hello everyone, my name's Emma. I'm going to show you round today.'

'Not Emma Woodhouse, surely,' Mr Sole thinks he's *so* hilarious.

Emma smiles, though she's obviously heard it before, 'No, I'm not Emma Woodhouse or Emma Knightley.'

'But are you single though, miss?' shouts Mathew Relf.

'Mathew,' his mum looks furious.

'Not really relevant,' says Emma with a smile, but Mr Sole is shaking his head.

'No shouting out, and sensible questions only,' he says, 'do remember you're representing Portsmouth City Comprehensive.'

Portsmouth City Dump, more like.

Emma then gives a talk about Jane Austen's life at Chawton. 'This house was provided by her brother, Edward, who owned nearby Chawton House, which you can also visit. It's a much grander residence with a large hall for entertaining and a well-stocked library which Jane would often visit.

'It was a great relief for Jane to have this house at Chawton and it enabled her to concentrate on her writing. It was here during the last eight years of her life that she revised *Pride and Prejudice*, *Sense and Sensibility* and *Northanger Abbey*, and also wrote *Mansfield Park*, *Emma* and *Persuasion*.'

Emma takes us back out into the courtyard, round the back and through the front door which is at the side and probably wasn't the front door in Austen's day. We file through the shop and I'm watching Janine. Her left hand can't help reaching out to touch a Regency-style bonnet, and a Chawton eraser, and I can see she's really tempted by a quill – just like Jane used to use – but thankfully she places it back down.

Emma talks us through a Jane Austen timeline, detailing the big events Austen lived through; then it gets more interesting: a lock of hair, a ball and cup, ivory dominoes and Jane's silhouette. She really lived here. She really lived.

'And this is where she wrote,' says Emma, as we enter a lovely square room with a window of small-paned glass. And that is where she sat, by the window at a tiny wooden desk.

'Bit small, innit,' says Mathew Relf.

'That's all she needed,' says Emma, and then she tells us about the door and shows us how it creaks. 'Jane Austen wouldn't let anyone oil or mend the door, she liked to have a warning if her writing was about to be disturbed.'

Upstairs, we see the room where she slept and then there are the clothes, the tiny clothes.

'You are joking me?' says Chantal Thomas, her arms folded, as we stare at the mannequins dressed in Jane Austen's printed muslin dresses.

'Jane Austen wore that? I was bigger than that when I was eleven.'

A few people nod in agreement. Chantal Thomas has always been tall.

'I'm nearly six foot now,' she says, 'I've been scouted by Models One.'

'Oh, very impressive,' says Emma, 'but I have to say, I doubt any woman was as tall as you in Austen's day. You see, people weren't as well nourished as we are today. Okay, I'm going to take you out to the gardens now and we'll have a look at the kitchen and laundry.'

Everyone starts to move, shuffling down the stairs in a long, snaking line and out of the back door, but I don't want to go. There's something about this place. I want to stay and try to feel Jane Austen's presence. I can't do that with my schoolmates around so I hang back, check no one's noticed, and then scoot back into Jane's writing room.

I can see her there sitting at the window, watching friends and neighbours and the world in general all passing by until she focuses in on her work in progress and her characters: Emma, Harriet, Mr Elton and Knightley—

She had it sussed – positioned herself perfectly. She could take in both the outside and inside, whoever was coming through the door. It's all so simple. She had all she needed – a quiet little life and yet so much to say.

'*Lucy, there you are*, I've been looking for you,' Mr Sole is frowning. 'You upset my headcount. I couldn't think who was missing, and then I realised it was you *yet again*.'

'Sorry, sir, I just wanted to have another look.'

Mr Sole stops, his frown fades away. 'And what is it you see, Lucy?'

He's really interested, waiting to hear, waiting as long as it takes.

I look back at the room, from door to desk to window.

'I see that you need only a little space, a tiny desk and a creaky door.'

❧

My inspiration: Having visited the Jane Austen Museum at Chawton twice, once as a child and once as an adult with my own family, I wanted to look at how learning about Austen's life, where she lived and how she worked could inspire someone young.

WE NEED TO TALK ABOUT MR COLLINS

Mary Howell

WE NEED TO TALK ABOUT MR COLLINS

※

Mary Howell

'Cup of tea, Charlotte? Black isn't it?'

'Lovely,' Charlotte smiled. They were practically friends. Eliza, the only woman she would trust to cut her hair, wayward curls that needed a firm hand. Charlotte smiled again before retreating under the pile of glossy magazines and the noise of the blower and a good half hour's staring. Weekly trips to *Thin Lizzie's* on the high street were the highlight of her quiet life; a constant round of light dusting, light shopping, light gardening, light strolls. Here, in Eliza's capable, manicured hands, she had her light trim, light set and, very occasionally, low lights to mask the incipient grey.

She found going to the hairdresser very pleasing. Nothing was expected of her as she sat inventing lives and intrigues for the other ladies reflected there and listening to the lop-sided conversations half drowned by mechanical sounds. The mirror in the salon was a perfect medium, allowing her to see the world yet to see only its reflection refracted many times, multifaceted yet flat like the pages of novels.

'Thought I'd buy ready-made and pass it off, save all that slog in the kitchen. Anyway I've clients till half six.' Eliza's hands-free phone was on constantly.

None of the ladies ever complained of inattention, so grateful perhaps to have a decent hairdresser in the village. She was pulling out curlers from the woman two seats down, running her hands through the fine grey, her red nails disappearing and reappearing rhythmically, repeatedly down the salon in smaller and smaller versions.

'Do you want hairspray, Gladys?'

The can was out in a flash, perhaps Gladys had commented on the windy day. Charlotte watched the slack lips move in the mirror but could not make out what they said. She imagined the hiss of the can and saw the cloud of fine spray.

Yes, definitely a hairspray day.

'She's not wearing hairspray.'

'Oh yes she is,' and workmen looking meaningfully into the young girl's shopping basket and seeing Harmony.

'A face without a trace of make-up.'

Charlotte laughed out loud and Eliza turned and smiled. Charlotte could meet her eyes in the mirror and see the woman's lips move wordlessly in front of Eliza's smile and the little black microphone in front of her teeth.

'Well you make it then if you're so bothered.'

Charlotte imagined the other end of the line. A husband, athletic, handsome in an earthy way with a broad back that would ripple under Eliza's red nails, who loved Eliza's no nonsense approach to life. Perhaps this was an important business supper and the husband needed to impress in order to make that step up the ladder.

'If I don't die of boredom I'll kill you for inviting him.'

She could not help feeling that Eliza should be a little more sympathetic to the needs of her husband and his associate. She could see her impudently picking her nails with her teeth at the table, fidgeting one slim leg over the other with a scrape of black stockings, to distract the men from their serious discussions. She was sure that, in Eliza's shoes, she would be more sensitive, she would know instinctively what was needed.

'A whole evening of Mr Collins would be fatal.'

The name made her focus and she was not often called in to the real world. For a delightful moment she imagined the clatter of a carriage, the rustle of silk and the appearance of the rector and his patron. She felt there was a place for her somewhere in the pages of this novel. Why else had she been christened Charlotte? The unmarried daughter of respectable, elderly parents now deceased, leaving their unmarried elderly daughter comfortably off but elderly and unmarried.

She was hot under her blower, with an uncomfortable sense that time had dislodged and been lost somewhere.

'Thanks very much, Gladys.'

The cash till registered with a ching, and a welcome rush of cool air as the door opened and closed, then relief when Eliza turned off the machine.

'Think you're cooked, Charlotte. You're all pink.'

Curlers dropped one by one onto the waiting trolley with a little click and Charlotte's hair recoiled.

'You'll have to ask someone else as well.' Eliza sounded almost petulant.

'Call me back will you.' Eliza moved the mouthpiece above her head. It looked like a hover fly, Charlotte thought.

'I could come and entertain Mr Collins for you.'

She laughed at her reflection, face to face with the multiple reality of it, pleased that the words were spoken. It was quite short notice, but with her hair done, no need to worry on her account, Mr Collins would do all the talking.

It had never been her intention to be a heroine, a romantic lead, but she thought, given an evening in the company of Mr Collins, even she could persuade him. She longed to be part of that world, any world, to join the sorority of married women whose bliss and trials she read about so often. At least, she thought she did until she got to the happy ending. Much as she enjoyed happy endings she could not trust them. They were a failing in novels, in life, a blind alley, a cul-de-sac; their inevitability ruined many pages, many days. She often did not finish books for that very reason, preferring to leave endless possibilities.

Charlotte noticed that Eliza did not stop to run her hands over her head in that satisfying way she usually did but seemed to punish the curls with her brush.

She was looking quite out of character, her mouth knitted in a tight knot of disapproval as she worked deftly, methodically. The salon with just the two of them seemed cold. There was tension in the spray that landed finely on her hair that Eliza had not offered and she had not accepted.

A border had been crossed: the fine line of professional and personal. Charlotte saw in her reflected pink face all the what-ifs of her life, the if-onlys, the wasted possibilities and was on the verge of falling into the bleak emptiness of it.

'Know what, Charlotte? I think you should come and meet Mr Collins.'

The emptiness receded.

Eliza tweaked at her fringe, bending her knees to get closer then put her head next to Charlotte's, resting her hands on her shoulders and fixing her eyes on the reflection.

'Like seafood?'

All of a sudden, the weight of Eliza's hands was unbearable. She saw for the first time how shrewd her eyes were; how calculating and she wanted to brush them off, free herself from the eyes, the salon and the whole sorry business. The impudence of the headset. Why should she, Charlotte Lucas of independent means and a comfortable home, entertain ideas of marrying?

'Who is Mr Collins?' her reflection asked. She could see she had recovered her usual pallor and poise.

Eliza took her hands from Charlotte's shoulders, pulled down the mouthpiece, still hovering, and listened. The salon was very still. Charlotte wondered if she should get up from her chair. She was ready to go home now.

A high snivelling sound came from Eliza. Tears were falling from her eyes.

'Well be like that, you bastard.'

A new chapter, a new book even. Charlotte thought she was letting herself down and pretended not to hear for as long as possible. Then it occurred to her that this was drama, a real-life drama reflected in the mirror before her.

'Is there anything—' Charlotte let the words trail, seeing herself in the mirror, the older but still attractive woman lending her worldly wisdom to the jilted youngster crying into her headset. Was the young man still there? Was he feeling remorse for his harshly spoken words? Not a bit of it, Charlotte decided. He would be brutish and arrogant and gone. Tears would not melt his heart. 'I hate it when you cry. Whatever you cook and whoever you chose to invite will be wonderful.' That type of happy ending was reserved for the type of books she did not read. Not to the end, at least.

Distinction blurred; a car door banged and the door to the salon was flung open with force such that it hit the wall. A man stood in the doorway, smiling. With the setting sun behind his head like a halo, he strode towards Eliza and taking her in his manly arms—

'Charlotte, Charlotte,' she heard her name repeated and felt a sharp tapping on her hand. He had come to take her for the meal of ready-made food. Her Mr Collins, whose presence Eliza could not endure for one evening.

A handsome young man in uniform was kneeling beside her holding her wrist.

'Please do not kneel.' Her words, though fully formed in her head, sounded jumbled.

'Can you hear me?'

What a ridiculous question. Then she remembered that was what is said at disasters when the hero or heroine is dying. 'Well, I'm not dying.' Again the words did not come.

Eliza was still tearful, 'She came over all, well, you know, and just slumped in my chair. I thought she had fallen asleep, she often does, but when she wouldn't wake up I thought I'd better call you.'

'You did the right thing, people often leave it too late and don't want to bother us. We'll take care of her. Do you know of any relative we can contact? I think it best to take her in.'

'Lives on her own – as far as I know she's an old maid.'

It dawned on Charlotte that they were speaking about her: she was the old maid. She would have liked to check the role in the mirror to see if it suited her noble profile but her head was so heavy she thought she would leave it for now. She was tired of the effort of life, tired of pretence. They had come to take her away, the fear of the old and lonely. Perhaps this is what happened in all those endings she had refused to read. It would be a new chapter in her life, hospital she supposed, for this was not the usual story. Perhaps she would be home again, back to her light, gentle life full of empty days, and that would do for the end.

Then Eliza, her practical friend, was beside her with her head close to hers.

'This gentleman is Mr Wickham. He thinks it best to take you in.'

None of it made much sense to Charlotte and she was in no mood to be taken in, certainly not by Mr Wickham. He had already taken in enough people when what everyone needed was truth and plain speaking.

'We may as well carry her; she only looks two scraps of nothing.'

Charlotte would have liked to look to see who they were talking about now, but she could not focus.

'Charlotte, I want you to put your arms round my neck, I'm going to take you—'

She felt the muscles taut across his shoulders and he lifted her as if she were no more than a feather. She laid her head on his shoulder and felt the stiff cloth of his uniform on her cheek. His smell was essence of man, of horse leather and fields and cigar smoke. It was pure Mills and Boon. Her mother had always warned her against filling her head with romantic nonsense but she felt the time had come to let herself go, 'Why, Mr Wickham.'

※

My inspiration: I wanted to write something giving minor characters a major role. I thought of Charlotte as the anti-heroine marrying the unfortunate Mr Collins so that at least she would have a modicum of independence. The thought of Mr Collins immediately made me want to laugh so the story would be droll. I love *Pride and Prejudice* but wanted a story that did not work out.

BINA

Andrea Watsmore

BINA

Andrea Watsmore

She could be sitting right next to them and they wouldn't notice her; the teachers, the boys, the other girls. She could slip into class wearing a menstrual red jumper that brought out the grey umbers and ochres in her skin, and that pulled tight across her small peachy breasts and still they wouldn't see her.

She was the only girl amongst us who could slowly peel a banana and bite into its flesh without the boys drooling at her. She was pretty though. Everything in the right place. And when she spoke, when she bothered, it was usually to say something considered. Not timid, like you might expect.

Then one day, I watched Mr Burdage pull her to one side at the end of Art, period three. He asked her what she wanted to do with her life. She held his eye and told him: lawyer.

Is that something you want to do, or something your family wants for you, because you have a talent in art, have you thought about studying it further?

And she smiled and asked him: was art something his family had wanted him to do?

He turned cerise and got excited and said: you know it's all going to become clear to you at university. The different ways you can live. There will be more people who...get you. Then he turned and scurried back into his art room.

Everyone knew that I liked Mani Burdage. He had never asked me what I wanted to do with my life, even though he knew that I wanted to go to Art School. He also knew that my dad was against the idea but that I wasn't going to let that stop me. We would be good together, Mani and me. I dreamt of living and working with him in his studio. Maybe even marrying. We would be a partnership, like Gilbert and George. Or open a shop and make and sell our work like Tracey Emin and Sarah Lucas did in the nineties.

Seeing as how Mani saw something interesting in Bina, I decided to adopt her; keep your rival close, they say. Also I was confident that I would look well next to her. That once I had brought her out of herself, she wouldn't appear layered and mysterious to him. She would be just the same as everyone else. Besides I was short on friends at the time.

This was our final year at Aloysius, so I had to act now. I decided to follow him, to see where he hung out. I knew where his studio was. I'd been there in September. He worked there on Saturdays, Sundays and on Wednesdays, his day off. It took a couple of days to persuade Bina to come with me. At first she pretended she didn't like him. Went all wide-eyed, *he's old enough to be my father*, at me. But I explained to her that he was only seven years older than us. That you had to see beyond the beard. Look at the thickness of his eyelashes; it's as if he wears mascara. See how unusual his dark blue eyes are against his green-gold skin. Watch his quick and clever hands when he draws. Feel his energy.

I wore her down in art. I threatened to tell Mani that she fancied him unless she came with me. Mani sealed it by asking us what all the fast talk and giggling was about. I looked at Bina, her name already formed on my lips and she held her hands up and said: okay, okay, I'll come. He became nervous around us after that. Kept giving us these fluttering pretty side-looks.

Late the following Saturday afternoon we sat in my mum's Honda watching his studio. I had parked it on a raised slip road at the back. From this position the area looked worse than I'd remembered. I could tell that Bina was not impressed; she was quiet, but not in that comfortable way of hers. The studios must have been ordinary offices once, perhaps for tax inspectors or telesales; row on top of row of balconied windows, punctuated with faded mustard panelling. Retro, but not in a good way. Many of the windows were boarded up. There were plants crushed against the glass on the inside and climbing green leaves coming through from the outside. Like *Romeo and Juliet*, only squalid. Perhaps if we had come at night, or if it had been a sunny day it might have looked better. The wall that half hid the skip-sized bins had been painted three shades of blue. Someone had graffittied a face with huge teeth and red and white eyes on it. Underneath they had written, <u>Mine, all mine</u>. I took my phone out to snap it. Bina said: you're not taking a picture of it? It's horrible. It's not Banksy, you know. It's just a crap drawing on a nasty wall using the paint left over after they'd finished decorating their bedrooms.

I had to photograph it then. Besides Banksy's first stuff wouldn't have been great either. Everyone starts somewhere. I opened the window to lean out. The stench outside was gagging. It stuck and clung in your nose and throat. Bina leant across me shrieking and hit my button to close it. The smell was inside now.

A thick, heavy green fug. We started to laugh.

I tried to explain Mani's work to Bina. At his private view there had been two video monitors each showing the head and shoulders of a different woman. They were both talking, one at a time, as if in a conversation, but what they were saying didn't add up. They were isolated in these screens, not able to listen or respond to each other.

Bina shook her head: so, he's trying to make the point that some people don't get other people? That they don't listen to what the other person is saying? Don't we know that already?

I told her that there was other stuff, drawings and these hankies embroidered in lilac with random words: *war treats, stone room, extra bullet*. And that also to get into his studio you had to walk under a ladder. This was part of the work, a funny joke, playing with people's superstitions and prejudices. I didn't tell her that although he had invited everyone in his year thirteen class, I was the only one who had gone. That Mani hadn't spoken to me until I was about to leave. Then he asked me to spell out my name for him, as if he didn't know me: Emma I Dunsley. He scribbled it down in this little square-lined notebook and then laughed, delighted. He told me, I'm collecting anagrams and yours is *unseemly maid*. Thing was, Bina didn't have to get it, because this wasn't the world she wanted to be part of.

I told her that we couldn't sit here in this smell. Who knows how long we would have to wait, even assuming he was in there. We would have to go inside and find him. Then she could judge his work for herself and we could see how he reacted to each of us. Bina got into a tizz and grabbed my hand and said, I can't go in there. We were both laughing and she pumped my hand and told me: you can't go in there, because...because...that smell is the smell of dead teenage girl. Mani lures them here and molests them, peels them alive and stitches their skin into canvases. And out of their bones he sculpts the finest, most beautiful miniature animals with his clever hands. Their entrails he just chucks in the bins with the KFC boxes.

I told her that that was the longest sentence that I'd ever heard her speak. She turned her face away and flashed her cobalt-black hair at me. I reached into it and felt the weight of it. It was thick; each piece of hair, not just the volume of it. I plucked a strand, wound it round my finger and told her that you could use her hair to sew with, it was so strong. Then I buried my face in it. It was just washed and the sweet chemicals were so strong that they obliterated everything else. I whispered to her that Mani is a conceptual artist. He doesn't do sculpting and painting. That he doesn't have the balls to do something as wild as that. I grabbed her left hand back and laid it on my palm. It was tiny, like a child's, but puffy and red like an old hag's. I told her this and she laughed so hard, she started to snort. So I told her that she snorted like a man. And she pulled her hand back and acted all offended: a man? A man? Not even a pig?

I thought I might have gone too far, so I put my lips against her stomach and burrowed and blew into it. I asked her to forgive me, told her that she was the most beautiful girl ever, more beautiful than Shilpa Shetty, hair more lovely than Amy Winehouse, eyes prettier than Mani Burdage— We were squealing and laughing so much it took us ten seconds to register the tapping sound on the glass.

The light had slipped since we had been sitting here and there was a face pressed against the window. We screamed and jumped and held on to each other's flesh. The figure reeled back like a frightened child. It was Mr Burdage. He waved both hands at us. I dropped Bina, turned my back on her and pressed the window down. I leaned out and filled the space, putting myself between Mani and Bina, so he could see only me.

I held his eyes and started to talk. I could feel him trying to look past me, but I told him we were looking for the Moustache Bar, that it was near here and that because we couldn't find it we were about to come in to the studios and ask someone. He gave me his down-turned smile, pretended that he believed the story and said no, he had not heard of that one. What sort of bar was it? Then he said we could try *Persuasion,* on the High Road. It seemed to be popular with a young crowd. Then he looked at his watch and said. It's a bit early, though. I asked him if he goes there. And he said, not me, I'm too old for that. Then he backed away from us. When he was at a safe distance, he moved his finger as if he was scribbling lines between us and said: I'm glad you two found each other. I called after him and asked him what the smell was. He looked confused and said, do you mean the canal?

Bina didn't say anything on the drive home. I asked her if we should try that bar. She shrugged and said that she had to get home. She was scratching a lot. Her hands, her arms, around her stomach.

In the end I said, Mani Burdage is all right, but he isn't worth peeling your skin off for. She covered her mouth in an affected way and then leaving one finger across her lips she looked at me and said: I was never interested in Mr Burdage. I don't know what interested me here.

I almost went after her when she left the car. But what could I say to her? Wasn't it a shame that he came over when he did, because for a moment there I thought we were going to kiss and I ached all over and this was so pure that the words shouldn't be spoken or embroidered or played with, and now I feel bruised and I want to sit rigid looking into her eyes, not even touching and then fall asleep wrapping myself in her hair and when we wake we are so entangled that we don't know where Bina ends and Emma begins. And this wouldn't be a partnership, a convenience. It would be everything.

My inspiration: In writing 'Bina' my starting point was Jane Austen's *Emma,* a character whose comic meddling and ambitions set off a chain of events that transform her and allow her to find the love that was there all along. My Emma is the narrator of the story.

Biographies

Lane Ashfeldt grew up in Ireland and England, and has lived and worked in several European countries. She is working on a collection of short stories. Her ambition is to live in the past; somewhere sufficiently far back for there to be no mobile phones or speaking buses, but not so far back that chalk gets passed off as food. Information about areas of Europe with permanent network voids gratefully received – contact Lane via her website www.ashfeldt.com.

Esther Bellamy is 28 and lives and farms in Hampshire. She read history at Oxford and worked at the House of Commons before studying land management at Cirencester Agricultural College. Between chasing beef cattle and avoiding paperwork she is studying for a Masters in Research in English at Southampton University where she is writing her thesis on the concept of failure in the novels of George Eliot. She is working on a novel. She reads omnivorously and a trail of destruction at the back of her house indicates that she may recently have taken up gardening as a hobby.

Kelly Brendel was born in 1989 in South London. She is currently a student at the University of York studying English Literature.

Suzy Ceulan Hughes was born in England but has lived in mid-Wales since 1977. She is a writer, translator and book reviewer. This is her first short story to be published.

Beth Cordingly was born in Brighton and attended Birmingham University where she gained a double first in English and Drama. She is currently doing the MA in Creative Writing at Birkbeck. She is a founding member of Nomads, a writers' workshop and of Lou's Crew, who are working on a comedy series for television. She is an established television and theatre actress.

Felicity Cowie is a former BBC Panorama journalist and a student on the MA in Creative Writing course at Bath Spa University. She is currently finishing her first novel and wrote 'One Character In Search Of Her Love Story Role' whilst developing the central character of Hannah Peel.

Felicity was longlisted for the Fish International Short Story Prize 2006 and, as a teenager, won the WH Smith Young Writer of the Year Competition. As a journalist, her most interesting guest was Buzz Aldrin.

Elaine Grotefeld was born in Montreal, Canada and grew up in the UK, where she read English at Jesus College, Cambridge. She wrote two of her dissertations on her favourite writer, Jane Austen (the second to attempt reparation for the first). Since then she's lived and worked in London, Vancouver, Hong Kong and Singapore – where she 'headhunted' technology executives by day and wrote poems, short stories and her novel by night. Happily squeezed between mountains and sea, Elaine is now back in Vancouver – with her Scottish husband, two children, and the occasional rummaging bear. *Persuasion's* theme of long-lost love inspired Elaine's short story 'Eight Years Later,' as well as her first and almost-cooked novel, *Meeting Joe McManus.*

Jacqui Hazell was born in Hampshire in 1968. She studied textile design at Nottingham and has had a range of humorous greetings cards published. She has also been a runner-up in the Vogue Talent Contest for young writers and worked briefly as a secretary at Buckingham Palace. She is a journalist and magazine editor and is currently studying for an MA in Creative Writing at Royal Holloway. Her first novel is entitled, *The Flood Video Diaries*. She lives in London.

Elizabeth Hopkinson usually finds her imagination veering towards the fantastic, and is therefore very pleased (and a little surprised) to find herself doing so well with a (nearly) straight story. She lives in Bradford, West Yorkshire, where she finds an endless source of inspiration in the coffee shop in the old Wool Exchange. Her stories have appeared in several genre magazines, webzines and anthologies, and her themed collection of 12 short stories, *My True Love Sent to Me*, is available from Virtual Tales. Her website is: www.hiddengrove.pwp.blueyonder.co.uk

Mary Howell was born with many advantages, most of which she turned her back on.

Educated to be a lady at a private convent, she excelled at truancy, managing only to achieve a fistful of star A levels. Her university career and her nursing career both ended abruptly with spells in prison. Both times she was released without stain.

She has lived all over the world, with as many aliases as lovers, She has been an orthodontist's assistant, a serial absconder, sawn in half by a magician and a happily married mother of three. She now lives in North Wales.

Clair Humphries graduated with a BA Hons in English Literature. She has worked in the Official Publications Reading Room of the British Library and is currently employed at a London university, where she provides support for disabled and dyslexic students. She writes humorous contemporary fiction and lives in Kent with her husband, Steve.

Kirsty Mitchell is 25 and was born in Ayr on the west coast of Scotland. She now lives in Glasgow. Her short stories have previously been published in *Mslexia* magazine, and placed in the Cadenza Short Story Competition, Frome Festival Short Story Competition, and the Bristol Short Story Prize. She is a graduate of Philosophy and History at Glasgow University.

Victoria Owens worked first in the book trade and later as a legal executive before reading for an English degree. PhD research on John Dryden's translation of the *Aeneid* followed; she finished her thesis about ten days before her eldest daughter's birth. She wrote her first novel when her younger daughter started playgroup and her second on Bath Spa University's MA in Creative Writing, but neither has found a publisher. Victoria runs and swims to keep fit, enjoys choral singing and belongs to the Gaskell Society. She lives near Bristol.

Penelope Randall was born in Leicester. She grew up in Norfolk and Nottinghamshire and, for three teenage years, in the Bahamas. She read Engineering Science at Oxford University and has worked as a civil servant, editor, typesetter and playgroup assistant. She currently teaches science and maths and wants to start a campaign against education buzzwords. She has always loved writing stories, and recent successes (and near-misses!) encourage her to hope that her three novels may one day find a publisher. She lives in Manchester.

Nancy Saunders lives in a Hampshire village and works in Library Aquisitions, sending out lovely new books to hungry readers. Writing, fiddle-playing and enjoying the great outdoors are all squeezed in around the job. Nancy is a past member of Alex Keegan's Bootcamp online writing group – without which her writing would not have won a couple of prizes and appeared in various publications. Elly and Oscar are Nancy's two true significant others.

Stephanie Shields was brought up in the Midlands but has spent all of her adult life in the north of England, where she has combined sheep farming with a career in further education. She has written poetry since childhood, but short fiction is a more recent development. Having had some early publication of her poetry in the 1970s, she has continued as a covert writer. She is a member of the Otley Courthouse Writers, based in the market town of Otley, West Yorkshire.

Elsa A. Solender, a New Yorker, was president of the Jane Austen Society of North America from 1996-2000. Educated at Barnard College and the University of Chicago, she has worked as a journalist, editor, and college teacher in Chicago, Baltimore and New York. She represented an international non-governmental women's organisation at the United Nations during a six-year residency in Geneva. She has published articles and reviews in a wide variety of American magazines and newspapers, but 'Second Thoughts' is her first published story. She has been married for 49 years, has two married sons and seven grandchildren.

Hilary Spiers lives in Stamford, Lincolnshire, works in adolescent health policy part-time and writes every day, when time and life permit. She has won a number of national writing competitions, been published in several anthologies and had some of her stories broadcast on the radio. Her abiding passion remains playwriting, for stage and radio. Her play *Hoovering on the Edge* was staged by Shoestring Theatre in September 2009 and she has had work performed at London's Hampstead Theatre and the Oundle Literature Festival. While collecting rejection letters, she acts in and directs other writers' plays.

Stephanie Tillotson joined the BBC in 1989 and worked in television and radio for many years, at length crossing to the independent sector in Wales. For the past ten years she has been writing, directing and performing for the theatre. Originally from Gilwern near Abergavenny, she now lives in Aberystwyth, where she has been teaching in the Department of Theatre, Film and Television Studies at the university. At present she is editing a book of short stories for Honno called *Cut on the Bias*, a collection of fictional writing about women's relationship to clothes and image.

Andrea Watsmore was born in the London/Essex borders in 1966, has four children and a Fine Art degree from Chelsea School of Art. This has led to a number of opportunities including usherette, engineer, tote operator, teacher, shop girl, bag lady and artist.

She has always written, whether in paintings or on lonely walls. Now she generally limits it to a spiral-bound notebook and laptop. 'Bina' is her first published story.

The Judges

Sarah Waters was born in Pembrokeshire. She has won a Betty Trask Award, the Somerset Maugham Award and was twice shortlisted for the *Mail On Sunday* / John Llewellyn Rhys Prize. *Fingersmith* and *The Night Watch* were both shortlisted for the Man Booker and Orange Prizes, and *Fingersmith* won the CWA Ellis Peters Dagger Award for Historical Crime Fiction and the *South Bank Show* Award for Literature. *Tipping the Velvet, Affinity* and *Fingersmith* have all been adapted for television. Her latest novel The Little Stranger, was published by Virago in 2009. She lives in London.

Lindsay Ashford is a former BBC journalist and the author of four published crime novels. Her second, *Strange Blood*, was shortlisted for the Theakston's Old Peculier Crime Novel of the Year Award. She has had short stories published and broadcast on BBC Radio 4 and has edited two collections of short fiction and prose for Honno: *Written In Blood* and *Strange Days Indeed*. She splits her time between a home on the Welsh coast and Chawton House, where she is a PR consultant.

Mary Hammond started her career writing historical novels for an American book packager in the early 1980s. She is now Senior Lecturer in Nineteenth-Century Literature at the University of Southampton, specialising in book history, and convenor for Southampton's MA in Creative Writing. She is the author of numerous books and articles on the print culture of Victorian Britain and has also written on contemporary creative writing.

Rebecca Smith is the five-times great niece of Jane Austen (descended from Jane's brother Frances, through his daughter Catherine Ann, who was born at Chawton House). She is a Teaching Fellow in Creative

Writing at Southampton University. Her first novel, *The Bluebird Café,* was published by Bloomsbury in 2001. Other novels are *Happy Birthday and All That* (Bloomsbury 2003) and *A Bit Of Earth* (Bloomsbury 2006).

Janet Thomas is a freelance editor, living in Aberystwyth. She has edited a wide range of books, including four short-story anthologies for Honno: *Catwomen from Hell, The Woman Who Loved Cucumbers, Mirror Mirror* and *Safe World Gone,* which were co-edited with Patricia Duncker. She has published short stories and her children's picture book *Can I Play?* (Egmont) won a *Practical Pre-School* gold award.

Two hundred years ago Jane Austen made a momentous journey. On a July day in 1809 she set out from Southampton at the invitation of her brother, Edward. He had inherited the Manor of Chawton after being adopted by a wealthy, childless couple and had offered her a new home on his estate. On taking up residence there with her mother and sister, Jane did something she had felt unable to do for a very long time: she took up her pen and began working on a novel.

Her arrival in the Hampshire village marked the start of what was to be the most productive period of her literary life. Jane had begun writing many years earlier when her father was the vicar of Steventon. She had produced draft versions of three of her novels – including the manuscript that would eventually become *Pride and Prejudice* – before she reached the age of 25. But her father's sudden decision to retire and go to live in Bath greatly upset his daughter. Leaving the house where she had been born and seeing her father's extensive book collection sold off, along with many other family possessions, plunged her into depression and effectively disabled her as a writer.

The following decade was spent moving from one rented house to another, first in Bath and later – following her father's death – in Southampton. During this period the prolific output of fiction she had produced during the 1790s came to a grinding halt. It was only when her brother Edward offered her a permanent home in what had been the Bailiff's cottage on the Chawton estate that she found the peace and security she needed to flourish as a writer.

Sense and Sensibility, Pride and Prejudice, Emma and *Mansfield Park* were all published while she lived in the village. *Northanger Abbey* and *Persuasion* were published posthumously after her death at the age of just 41.

So the Great House, as Edward's Elizabethan mansion was known then, was inextricably linked with Jane Austen's destiny. Her brother provided an environment in which she could thrive and in those last fruitful years she would often make the short walk from her cottage to the grand building that rose above the parish church of Saint Nicholas.

Chawton House had a fine library that was an undoubted attraction to Jane. The house was also the setting for many Austen family gatherings: '…we four sweet Brothers and Sisters dine today at the Gt House. Is that not quite natural?' she wrote to her friend, Anna Lefroy.

The house has recently been restored to its former glory thanks to an American entrepreneur who is a devoted Austen fan. For centuries it was the comfortable country home of the Knight family (it was Thomas and Catherine Knight who adopted Jane's brother, Edward, and he subsequently changed his name to Knight). Following the First World War, however, it fell into decline due to inheritance taxes and ever-increasing running costs – the fate of many other country estates in England.

By 1987, when Richard Knight inherited the property from his father, it was on the verge of financial and physical collapse. Its long and distinguished history, from mediaeval manor to one of Hampshire's great country houses, seemed to be drawing to an end. Its associations with Jane Austen looked destined to become mere memories.

Five thousand miles away in California, Sandy Lerner, co-founder of Cisco Systems, Inc., learnt of this misfortune. Sandy had discovered Austen while under unbearable pressure as an undergraduate computer science student at Stanford. She read *Persuasion* and was instantly hooked (she has since read the book more than seventy times).

After floating Cisco in 1990, Sandy and her former husband, Len Bosack, had turned a large percentage of the proceeds over to a foundation dedicated to scientific research, animal welfare and literary endeavours. She realised that Chawton House could be the perfect home for her collection of books by the long-forgotten early English women writers who were Austen's literary mothers and sisters. In Sandy's vision, Chawton House would be the ideal environment for research and study in a manner that would bring to life the social, domestic, economic, cultural and historical context in which the writers lived and worked. In short, a unique opportunity to study the works in an appropriate setting.

From this resolve she acquired a long lease from Richard Knight and began an extensive programme of conservation work. The house reopened in 2003 as Chawton House Library – the world's first centre for the study of the lives and works of women writing in English before 1830. As well as an original manuscript and early editions of Jane Austen's work, authors such as Mary Shelley, Mary Wollstonecraft, Frances Burney and Aphra Behn feature in the collection of more than 8,000 books. The library is open by appointment to members of the public and there are visiting fellowships available for more specialised research.

The Jane Austen Short Story Award was initiated by Chawton House Library to encourage contemporary creative writing. The 2009 competition attracted nearly three hundred entries from all over the world. The hope is that two centuries on, a new generation of writers will be inspired by Jane's work and the Great House she knew so well.

Lindsay Ashford, July 2009

For more information about Chawton House Library, visit the website: www.chawtonhouse.org

The lighter side of HISTORY

ANNETTE VALLON:
A Novel of the French Revolution
by James Tipton
978-0-06-082222-4 (paperback)
For fans of Tracy Chevalier and Sarah Dunant comes this vibrant, alluring debut novel of a compelling, independent woman who would inspire one of the world's greatest poets and survive a nation's bloody transformation.

BOUND: A Novel
by Sally Gunning
978-0-06-124026-3 (paperback)
An indentured servant finds herself bound by law, society, and her own heart in colonial Cape Cod.

CASSANDRA & JANE: A Jane Austen Novel
by Jill Pitkeathley
978-0-06-144639-9 (paperback)
The relationship between Jane Austen and her sister—explored through the letters that might have been.

CROSSED: A Tale of the Fourth Crusade
by Nicole Galland
978-0-06-084180-5 (paperback)
Under the banner of the Crusades, a pious knight and a British vagabond attempt a daring rescue.

A CROWNING MERCY: A Novel
by Bernard Cornwell and Susannah Kells
978-0-06-172438-1 (paperback)
A rebellious young Puritan woman embarks on a daring journey to win love and a secret fortune.

DANCING WITH MR. DARCY:
Stories Inspired by Jane Austen and Chawton House Library
Edited by Sarah Waters
978-0-06-199906-2 (paperback)
An anthology of the winning entries in the
Jane Austen Short Story Award 2009.

DARCY'S STORY
by Janet Aylmer
978-0-06-114870-5 (paperback)
Read Mr. Darcy's side of the story—*Pride
and Prejudice* from a new perspective.

DEAREST COUSIN JANE:
A Jane Austen Novel
by Jill Pitkeathley
978-0-06-187598-4 (paperback)
An inventive reimagining of the intriguing
and scandalous life of Jane Austen's cousin.

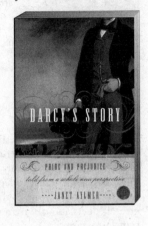

THE FALLEN ANGELS: A Novel
by Bernard Cornwell and Susannah Kells
978-0-06-172545-6 (paperback)
In the sequel to *A Crowning Mercy*, Lady Campion Lazender's courage,
faith, and family loyalty are tested when she must complete a perilous
journey between two worlds.

A FATAL WALTZ: A Novel of Suspense
by Tasha Alexander
978-0-06-117423-0 (paperback)
Caught in a murder mystery, Emily must do the unthinkable to save her
fiancé: bargain with her ultimate nemesis, the Countess von Lange.

FIGURES IN SILK: A Novel
by Vanora Bennett
978-0-06-168985-7 (paperback)
The art of silk making, political intrigue, and a sweeping love story all
interwoven in the fate of two sisters.

THE FIREMASTER'S MISTRESS: A Novel
by Christie Dickason
978-0-06-156826-8 (paperback)
Estranged lovers Francis and Kate rekindle their
romance in the midst of Guy Fawkes's plot to blow up
Parliament.

THE GENTLEMAN POET:
A Novel of Love, Danger, and Shakespeare's The Temptest
by Kathryn Johnson
978-0-06-196531-9 (paperback)
A wonderful story that tells the tale of how William Shakespeare may have come to his inspiration for *The Tempest*.

JULIA AND THE MASTER OF MORANCOURT: A Novel
by Janet Aylmer
978-0-06-167295-8 (paperback)
Amidst family tragedy, Julia travels all over England, desperate to marry the man she loves instead of the arranged suitor preferred by her mother.

KEPT: A Novel
by D. J. Taylor
978-0-06-114609-1 (paperback)
A gorgeously intricate, dazzling reinvention of Victorian life and passions that is also a riveting investigation into some of the darkest, most secret chambers of the human heart.

THE KING'S DAUGHTER: A Novel
by Christie Dickason
978-0-06-197627-8 (paperback)
A superb historical novel of the Jacobean court, in which Princess Elizabeth, daughter of James I, strives to avoid becoming her father's pawn in the royal marriage market.

THE MIRACLES OF PRATO: A Novel
by Laurie Albanese and Laura Morowitz
978-0-06-155835-1 (paperback)
The unforgettable story of a nearly impossible romance between a painter-monk (the renowned artist Fra Filippo Lippi) and the young nun who becomes his muse, his lover, and the mother of his children.

PILATE'S WIFE:
A Novel of the Roman Empire
by Antoinette May
978-0-06-112866-0 (paperback)
Claudia foresaw the Romans' persecution of Christians, but even she could not stop the crucifixion.

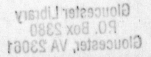

…RTRAIT OF AN UNKNOWN WOMAN: A Novel

…nora Bennett

9…-0-06-125256-3 (paperback)

Meg, adopted daughter of Sir Thomas More, narrates the tale of a famous Holbein painting and the secrets it holds.

THE PRINCESS OF NOWHERE: A Novel

by Prince Lorenzo Borghese

978-0-06-172161-8 (paperback)

From a descendant of Napoleon Bonaparte's brother-in-law comes a historical novel about his famous ancestor, Princess Pauline Bonaparte Borghese.

THE QUEEN'S SORROW: A Novel of Mary Tudor

by Suzannah Dunn

978-0-06-170427-7 (paperback)

Queen of England Mary Tudor's reign is brought low by abused power and a forbidden love.

REBECCA:
The Classic Tale of Romantic Suspense

by Daphne du Maurier

978-0-380-73040-7 (paperback)

Follow the second Mrs. Maxim de Winter down the lonely drive to Manderley, where Rebecca once ruled.

REBECCA'S TALE: A Novel

by Sally Beauman

978-0-06-117467-4 (paperback)

Unlock the dark secrets and old worlds of Rebecca de Winter's life with investigator Colonel Julyan.

THE SIXTH WIFE: A Novel of Katherine Parr

by Suzannah Dunn

978-0-06-143156-2 (paperback)

Kate Parr survived four years of marriage to King Henry VIII, but a new love may undo a lifetime of caution.

WATERMARK: A Novel of the Middle Ages

by Vanitha Sankaran

978-0-06-184927-5 (paperback)

A compelling debut about the search for identiy, the power of self-expression, and value of the written word.

Available wherever books are sold, or call 1-800-331-3761 to order.